The Viscount Deception

WENDY MAY ANDREWS

Sparrow Ink
www.sparrowdeck.com

ISBN - 978-1-989634-01-1

www.wendymayandrews.com

Sparks fly. Will they burn bridges or warm hearts?

After almost becoming a pawn in a villain's schemes, Lady Anne is firming her backbone and grasping independence. But that doesn't change the fact that she needs to make an advantageous marriage to pull her family out of destitution.

Confirmed bachelor, Wesley Dunbar, Viscount of Bracondale, is furious when he learns of her involvement in the plot against his best friend. But he's also mesmerized by Anne's transformation from a country duckling to a fierce and beautiful swan.

Wesley and Anne's ambitions couldn't be more different, so why can't they stay away from each other? Will they both be able to find what they seek by mending their differences and standing side-by-side?

Dedication

In this series Anne changes and grows more than any other character I've ever written, in my opinion. She realized she was on the wrong path and made adjustments. I think we all do this even more often than we realize. But when we're in the middle of it, it's tough. If you're in the midst of your own metamorphosis, this book is for you. May it give you a short break from your tough struggles and may it give you hope that you, too, will get to your happily ever after.

Acknowledgements

My beta readers are my support team and their help is invaluable! Thank you Marlene, Suzanne, Monique, Alfred, and Christina. I don't think I could do it without you.

My editor, Julie Sherwood, is a dream to work with. She tightens up my stories and fixes my blunders. Any mistakes remaining in the manuscript are my own.

This gorgeous cover was created by the skilled Josephine Blake of JB Designs.

A book cannot be complete without an acknowledgement to my husband. Without him I wouldn't even be on this journey. His dare made me write that first book and his support keeps me at my keyboard.

Chapter One

Watching the young woman circle the room in the arms of some aristocratic gentleman whose name he could not at the moment recall caused Wesley's ire to rise at an unreasonable rate. He knew he shouldn't feel so angry with her. She was just like nearly every other young woman in attendance. But unlike the other young women in attendance, she had tried to entrap his best friend into marriage so an amoral villain could gain control of the young duke. And that fact was what had Wesley so uncharacteristically angry.

As he stood on the side lines of the dance floor watching the debutantes and dandies, it crossed Wesley's mind that he really ought to leave. Feeling as he did, he doubted he would be able to make socially acceptable conversation that evening. Just as he was thinking that, as luck would have it, Lady Anne and her dance partner came to a stop right in front of him as the music slowed to silence momentarily. Wesley gritted his teeth and forced himself to smile politely as they bowed and curtsied to one another.

As the small orchestra struck up the next number, Wesley was shocked to hear his own voice asking, "Might I have the honour of this dance, my lady?"

The young woman nearly simpered as she dipped into a curtsy to him and accepted his proffered hand. "I would be delighted, my lord."

Wesley had to fight not to roll his eyes. He really wanted to walk away without dancing with her. He could not for the life of him fathom what had come over him to ask the wench to dance. He doubted it were within his power to be civil for the required four or five minutes that he would have to be in her company. Because, of course, it was not a country dance that would have given them breaks from each other as the steps were performed. No, it was a minuet. He would be stuck with the chit in his arms for a minimum of four minutes. He would have cheerfully lopped off his tongue in that moment if it would allow him to take back his impulsive words.

Wracking his brain for something innocuous to discuss, Wesley was at a loss when Lady Anne surprised him by asking the last thing he would have expected her to bring up. "Have you spoken to either Miss Smythe or the Duke of Wrentham?"

Wesley felt his hands tighten on her and saw the flicker of alarm cross her features. He could tell she was nervous. The young woman usually gave the appearance of a mouse. And while she still looked timid, he could see she was making every effort not to quail under what he was certain was a rather fierce glare from him.

Striving for a steady tone, Wesley asked, "Why would you ask me that?"

"Miss Smythe was one of the few women who seemed genuinely friendly towards me since I have come up to London with my father for the Season, so I wish her all the best. I do not know any details, but from something my father said to me, I know that she has encountered a bit of difficulty. I feel that I am somehow involved because of my father and his associate, so I thought to ask you if you know anything."

Wesley was struck with a torrent of conflicting feelings. He was quite aware the nervous young lady was making an effort to be brave, and a small part of him wanted to applaud her attempt. But the rest of him was furious that she would even dare to bring it up. She had brought a threat to two of his dearest friends, and that was not something he would readily forgive.

He heard the iciness in his tone and had no regrets as he answered her. "I have absolutely no desire to discuss this particular topic with you, my lady."

Her blue gaze dropped from his for a moment as a not unbecoming blush spread across her features. The viscount watched with a measure of appreciation as she took a deep breath and stunned him once again by meeting his eyes valiantly and baldly asking, "Why not?" There was an infinitesimal pause before she added, Wesley suspected sarcastically, "my lord."

Now he had to fight the urge to laugh at her obvious irritation. It was like watching a kitten getting mad at a guard dog. "Considering that any trouble my friends might be facing at the moment arrived at their doorstep via an association with you, I do not think you have any right to information about them at this juncture." Wesley could hear just how pompous he sounded but found he didn't care in the least. He waited to see how she would react to his statement.

Again, her eyes shifted away guiltily, and her cheeks maintained their high colour. He suspected she was wishing herself elsewhere, but she did not cave in. After another deep breath, she again dragged her gaze back to meet his, valiantly attempting to maintain her composure. "I am not in the custom of contradicting gentlemen, even when they are wrong, but I find that I shall have to make an exception this time, my lord."

Her tone was so shy and nervous that Wesley almost missed the meaning of her words. Swallowing a chuckle that threatened to emerge over her effrontery, Wesley forced himself to stare coldly into her timid blue gaze. "Was that convoluted statement supposed to mean that you think I am wrong?"

Watching her swallow nervously but hold his gaze while she nodded, Wesley began to feel like a bully for confronting her, but he was not yet prepared to back down from his position.

"I hardly think you are in any position to correct me, my lady. As you said, because of your father and his associate and their use of you to further their ends, trouble found my friends. I think you ought to leave it at that and be relieved that you have been preserved from feeling any consequences."

Wesley felt his first inkling of concern in that moment as her eyes flared with what he would have thought was anger on someone else, but he doubted the mousy Lady Anne ever felt anything that fierce in her life.

"You know nothing of my life, my lord. But you are quite correct. I am not in any position to censure you. Please forget that I asked, and let us merely enjoy the last moments of this lovely dance."

Contrarily, her mild acceptance of his refusal made Wesley want to discuss the matter further. Recognizing the musicians were bringing the minuet to a close, Wesley did the unthinkable. Bowing to his partner, he kept a firm hold on her hand. "Please, allow me to escort you to the refreshment room."

~~~

Anne gazed at him in amazement. The irritating man had just seconds prior appeared to heartily wish to be rid of her. Now, he seemed eager to prolong their interlude. Shaking her head, Anne once again arrived at the conclusion that men were irrational creatures. She tried to tug her hand from his grasp, but his grip was firm. "I am perfectly fine on my own, thank you, my lord." She tried to make her tone severe but doubted she had succeeded when he merely graced her with a benign smile and tucked her hand in his elbow.

Not wishing to draw attention to herself, Anne was forced to allow the insufferable man to keep her at his side. She knew she ought to be grateful. If word of the situation she had been trying to discuss with him ever got out, the fact that she had
~~~

been seen in his company would help dispel any rumours of her involvement. She knew the *ton* would not suspect her of any involvement if Lord Dunbar, the Viscount of Bracondale, was seen as being friendly with her. It was well known amongst the *ton* how deep the friendship of the Viscount of Bracondale and the Duke of Wrentham went. She tried not to be jealous. She would love to have that kind of friendship with someone. Or anyone. Of course, she had her dog, she reminded herself with a stab of homesickness. She missed the hairy sheepdog and wished she had been able to bring him to London, but her aunt wouldn't have allowed the hairy dog into the house. Too, Anne missed the lovely, loyal servants who remained on their rundown estate despite the irregularity of their wages.

She hadn't meant to let it out, but her soft sigh must have been audible as the viscount turned his sharp gaze on her. "Am I walking too fast for you, my lady?" She didn't trust his solicitous tone but answered him truthfully nonetheless. "My thoughts were elsewhere, my lord. I am perfectly able to keep up. Have no fear."

Anne almost smiled over the quizzical glance he cast her way before continuing toward the punch bowl. She remained at his side while they each accepted a glass of punch from the attentive servant. Just as she was about to take a sip, she felt the viscount tug her toward a vacant alcove. She was glad she hadn't managed to swallow anything as she would have no doubt choked with surprise as he said, "Let us take a seat over there for a moment."

"Whatever for, my lord? Surely you wish to be rid of me at the earliest opportunity." She pointed out what she thought was a reasonable statement.

"Not at all, my dear. Why would you say something so preposterous?"

Now, Anne actually felt genuine amusement for the first time in longer than she wished to remember, days at least, if not weeks. "Because you refused to answer the one question I most want to have answered. And your explanation for said refusal left little doubt in my mind that you have no wish to prolong your association with me."

Despite her discomfort, Anne could not hold her tongue. It was most unusual for her. She was used to being silent and keeping her few thoughts to herself. The Viscount of Bracondale had a most distressing effect on her. She really ought to insist that he allow her to return to the ballroom. Her intent must have been written upon her features because just as she was about to turn away from the chairs he was clearly guiding her toward, she felt the viscount's grasp tighten upon her elbow.

"Please, my lady, might I have just a few more minutes of your time?"

Anne found that she could not resist when the handsome lord turned such a sincere look upon her. She was quite certain the sincerity was feigned, but she allowed him to guide her to the seat he had indicated.

Gazing at him while she sipped her punch, Anne could see the hard look return to the viscount's face. She stifled another sigh. She should have known this was not going to be a pleasant interlude. A wave of longing for the simple life she had led with her father on their decaying estate swept through her, but she hurried to suppress the melancholy thoughts. As her father had pointed out to her, the estate was about to fall down around their ears. She had little hope of returning there. If she did not manage to contract an advantageous marriage, she was going to have to throw herself upon the charity of her relatives in order to have a roof over her head.

She really ought to be making an effort to turn the viscount up sweet. Rumour had it he was one of the wealthiest of the aristocratic bachelors. But looking into his cold, hard face, Anne could not muster any enthusiasm for the thought.

Looking around the room at the other milling guests, Anne tried to push all concerned thoughts from her mind and merely waited to hear what the viscount might next have to say.

~~~
~~~

"How can you sit there as though you have not a care in the world, my lady?" Wesley heard the exasperation in his tone but didn't care. He could not understand this woman in the least. Either she was a simpleton or she was a renowned actress. Neither was an acceptable option.

He watched in surprise as another delicate blush rose in her cheeks, but she lifted one shoulder in a negligent shrug. "I do not choose to acknowledge my cares while I am in public, my lord. It really would not be polite to have a fit of hysterics in the middle of a ball."

At this, Wesley lost control of his amusement and actually chuckled at her words, causing a few heads to turn and regard them curiously. He watched in fascination as the colour in her cheeks disappeared for a brief moment and then flooded back darker than before.

"My lord!" Her tone was scolding, but she said nothing else, merely gazing at him with a mixture of horror and fascination.

Wesley's laughter disappeared and they sat there in silence regarding each other seriously for a brief moment. He broke the strained silence. "Why do you really want to know about Alex and Rose?"

"I told you, my lord, I am concerned for Miss Smythe. I know there is nothing I could possibly do to help either of them, but I was actually hoping for reassurance that they shall be fine."

Her eyes didn't quite meet his, so Wesley doubted she was telling him the entire truth. He decided to probe the subject further. He could see that she was uncomfortable being in his presence and hoped that would prompt her to reveal something she would have otherwise kept to herself.

"What do you know of their situation?" he prompted.

"Very little, my lord. I really have no wish to discuss this with you. Could you just, please, tell me if Miss Smythe is all right?"

Wesley resisted the prodding of his conscience and his twenty-eight years of training as a gentleman. "I really do not feel as though I ought to tell you anything, my lady."

"Then why did you bother to prolong our time together?" Despite her obvious discomfort, she did not resist questioning him.

Wesley rewarded her flash of bravery with honesty. "I really have no idea. I am intensely angry with you for the trouble you brought upon them. It is the first time in my life that I have ever felt this way about a lady, and I do not know quite how to handle it."

He was surprised to see her blinking at him as though he had lost his mind. There was another brief silence before his surprise deepened when she spoke. "As I said before, my lord, I hesitate to contradict you, but I did not bring the trouble upon them. I may have been briefly a tool involved in this trouble, but I do believe Miss Smythe brought the trouble upon herself by getting involved in a matter that was not actually any of her business." There was another pause as she appeared to gather her composure and courage before continuing. "Now, would you please tell me if they are all right?"

Wesley regarded the female in front of him as though she were a curiosity at the fair. He could not make sense of her. It was obvious to him that she was terrified, but she refused to cower. He felt a kernel of respect start to germinate in his chest but shoved that to the back of his mind.

He decided he'd had enough of this particular conversation. He really ought not to have made any attempt to talk to the woman while he was unable to completely control his fuming anger. He took note of the fact that she had finished her glass of punch. He stood abruptly and grabbed her hand, pulling her to her feet beside him and curling her hand around his elbow.

"They shall be just fine," he finally answered curtly. "Now, shall I return you to the ball room?"

He felt her intent gaze burning into the side of his head, but he refused to meet her eyes, merely guiding her through the throngs of people as they headed in the direction of the music.

~~~

Before she quite knew what was happening, the viscount was bowing over her hand and taking his leave of her.

Anne felt almost bereft as the viscount walked away, which was ridiculous considering how haughtily he had treated her. She felt a crease of worry forming between her brows as she gazed at his retreating back. This would just not do. Smoothing the frown away with effort, Anne forced her thoughts to pleasant ones and her eyes back to the dance floor as another young man came to ask her to dance. With relief, she took his hand and stepped into the lively quadrille.

As she made her way through the familiar steps, she had the eerie feeling that someone was watching her. Ensuring that she kept her place in the dance, Anne allowed her gaze to dart about the dance floor in an attempt to ascertain who it might be. She almost tripped as her gaze collided with that of the Viscount of Bracondale. *Why is the infuriating man watching me?* she wondered with exasperation. Recovering her composure, she smiled pleasantly at her dance partner and forced her concentration on the steps while her mind scurried around the many questions plaguing her.

Her current dance partner was bowing over her hand just as Lord Spencer approached her. "My dear Lady Anne, would you do me the honour of sharing this next dance with me? It sounds as though they are striking up the waltz."

Anne felt warmth climb into her cheeks. She was quite aware there were many who questioned whether the waltz should be allowed in polite company. She had only danced it a handful of times herself. She could tell the earl was waiting for her reaction.
~~~

With an unconscious defiant lift of her chin, Anne put her hand in the earl's outstretched one. "I would be delighted," she replied, her polite tone not revealing how much she was looking forward to the dance. Lord Spencer, the Earl of Sutton, was rumoured to be a skilled dance partner, but she had not yet had the pleasure of dancing with him herself.

She tried not to get her hopes up about a potential match. The Earl of Sutton would be a remarkably good catch, but she didn't feel any snag of excitement as she stepped into his arms, despite the intimacy forced upon them by the waltz. It was strange. She had never thought that was important until the thrill she had felt in the viscount's arms.

As she circled the dance floor, she thought back to the conversation she'd had with Rose and another friend about the need to have love in marriage. While it was not strictly necessary, she knew quite well, it was a thought she was having difficulty getting out of her mind ever since that conversation. She had previously never considered the possibility of making a love match. It was rarely done in their circles, was even looked upon with a level of derision. But ever since the idea had been planted in her head, Anne had struggled uprooting it.

"So, what were you and Bracondale arguing about during your dance?"

Anne was startled out of her disquieting thoughts by the earl's question. She scrambled for an acceptable answer.

"I do not have any idea what you are talking about, my lord. Neither the viscount nor I would do something so ill bred as to argue in a crowded ballroom."

To her surprise, the earl graced her with a charming grin. "I suppose you are right. He always was rather fastidious about such things. But I must tell you, I have known him since we were boys, and it looked to me as though he *wanted* to argue with you, even if you were both too polite to do so." There was a brief pause while Anne looked at the earl with dismay and he watched her with careful assessment. "It piqued my curiosity, I must say."

Anne tilted her head in order to study his face carefully. It took her a moment to process his last statement but when she did, it took considerable effort not to burst into laughter. "Do I understand you to mean that you became highly interested in dancing with me when you thought that perhaps your friend wanted to argue with me?"

At his nod, she allowed a grin to crease her face. "Might I be so bold as to ask why?"

The earl shrugged and graced her with another grin of his own. "Like I said, I have known Bracondale for eons, since we were boys. Obviously, you don't know him that well or you would understand. The man is of a ridiculously sunny temperament. When we were boys, he would invariably find the bright side to look upon. It could be intolerably annoying when all you wanted to do was be angry about something. So, to see him looking on the verge of temper was a novel experience that must be explored. And since it would appear that it was directed towards you, I thought I would begin my investigation right here."

Feeling genuine amusement with the earl's statement but mistrusting the calculating gleam in his eyes, Anne merely offered a shrug of her own. "I cannot enlighten you, my lord. As I said, we did not argue. I cannot begin to fathom what his lordship might have been thinking. You shall simply have to ask him yourself."

She hoped her face didn't give away how nervous he made her as his eyes narrowed speculatively on her face, although she doubted much escaped the sharp-eyed Earl of Sutton. Anne was relieved a moment later when he gave a decisive nod as though declaring he was going to take her word for it, at least for the moment. But then he proceeded to confound her with his next question.

"Why is this the first time we have danced, my lady? You are an excellent dancer and reasonably pretty. I am certain I ought to have danced with you before now."

Anne couldn't help the gasp of laughter that escaped her at these unanswerable words. "I am unsure how to reply to such a statement, my lord."

"Oh, my dear, have I said something offensive? I have yet to learn to leash my wretched tongue."

"No, no, you did not offend me, my lord, have no fear. In the way of answering your question, I have not been in Town over long. Perhaps we have just not attended the same events. Have you been here for the entire Season?"

"I have. I am remarkably devoted to taking my seat in the House of Lords. That, of course, coincides with the Season. And as it seems I am always trying to convince someone to take my side on a particular argument, I have to attend his wife's ball or rout or whatever nonsense in order to gain his agreement."

Anne blinked at him for a moment before asking, "So what are you trying to get Lord Hudson to agree to, my lord?"

The earl grinned. "Well, I certainly couldn't entrust that sort of information to someone not involved, now could I?"

Feeling disgruntled, Anne grumbled, "You are the one who brought it up, my lord."

"You are quite correct and I apologize, my lady. That was not well done of me, was it? Now tell me, how have you been enjoying your first Season?"

Anne admired his skilled change of subject. Despite his occasional lack of tact, it was obvious he was firmly in control of his own social discourses. Her own proper upbringing forced her to politely answer his question.

"It has certainly had its ups and downs, my lord. It has not quite turned out as I had expected."

"What had you been expecting?"

Anne wished he had asked her about the weather rather than about the Season. She was unused to prevaricating but doubted he would appreciate her full honesty.

"I hadn't expected the crowds and the noise. I had no idea there would be quite so many people. I rather think I had not given the entire experience sufficient thought, to be honest, my lord. I naïvely thought I could show up, receive an offer of marriage, and carry on with my life comfortably."

To Anne's chagrin, Lord Spencer chuckled again, although, thankfully, this time he kept his volume low and it did not draw the eyes of others in the room. As Anne had pointed out, the vast crowds did tend to produce a great deal of noise. No one had noticed his laughter.

"How long have you been here, my lady?"

"Two and a half weeks."

"And you thought you would already be heading off to your husband's estate by now?" His incredulous tone brought heat to her cheeks, and Anne realized she had managed to reveal her foolishness. She gritted her teeth and tried to brazen it out. *This evening can hardly get worse*, she thought with a touch of desperation.

"Clearly, I was mistaken," she managed in a tone that, with relief, sounded unconcerned to her own ears.

Lord Spencer's sharp gaze was still focused on her face, but then his attention glided over her shoulder and his expression altered. "Tell me, Lady Anne, why the viscount is still watching you."

It took every ounce of will power she possessed not to crane around to see what the earl was looking at. Keeping her face as impassive as she could muster, Anne answered him as neutrally as possible. "I have no idea what you are talking about, my lord. My father is a viscount, is that who you are talking about? It would be reasonable for him to keep an eye on me, would you not agree?"

"Your father is not the viscount I meant, my dear, surely you realize that." Again the Earl of Sutton was looking at her as though he wished to read her mind.

Anne was overcome with relief when she heard the music dying away. "Thank you for the dance, my lord. It was pleasant." She kept her tone bland and was turning away when her relief died a quick death. The Viscount of Bracondale was standing next to them and appeared as though he were waiting for her.

"I believe this next dance is promised to me," the viscount declared. Without waiting for her reply, he swept her back onto the dance floor.

~~~

Wesley could see consternation glowing in the depths of Anne's eyes, but she managed to keep a serene expression on her face. He was beginning to suspect she was not nearly as empty headed as she let on.

"What did you and Sutton discuss?" he asked, trying to sound as though he were making idle chitchat.

"I do believe we were discussing you, my lord," Anne answered, her tone slightly breathless.

"You aren't certain one way or the other?" Wesley demanded.

"The earl strikes me as being a trifle strange, my lord. I do apologize for saying so, as he told me the two of you are particular friends, so I hesitate to insult a close companion of yours, but the entire encounter was decidedly peculiar."

"Why do you say that, my lady?" Wesley's curiosity was truly piqued, and he was looking forward to the insight into her character. His fascination only increased as he watched the blush climb in her cheeks once more. He chastised himself briefly. He really ought to leave the poor woman alone. She was obviously unused to such attentions.

"He seemed to be strangely fascinated with our previous dance, my lord." She paused for a moment, clearly reluctant to continue, but while he maintained his silence she plunged on. Wesley was surprised to find her clear gaze looking him straight in the eye as she demanded, "Are the two of you in some sort of competitive game involving me? I do not understand why you would each be questioning me about my conversation with the other."
~~~

Wesley realized with a slight start that the young woman in his arms was beginning to look angry. He felt the first stirrings of intrigue. She was quite obviously not the mousy little creature he had taken her to be. While she presented a façade of being a meekly acquiescent daughter to her broken down father, Wesley could see there really was a backbone hidden inside her delicate frame. He called himself to attention and addressed her question quickly when he saw the sparkle of tears brighten her eyes.

"No, no, of course not, my dear Lady Anne. I apologize profusely for giving you that impression. The earl and I have been friends since we were young lads at school. We have been like brothers since our young years. Like any brothers, we have a history of pulling pranks upon one another, but we also have always been fiercely loyal to one another. The Duke of Wrentham was one of our brethren. Sutton was, no doubt, like me, concerned over your possible connection with that trouble."

He watched with interest as Anne's gaze turned guilty for a moment, but then she met his eyes frankly. "I have my doubts about that, my lord, as he did not make any reference to the duke. He seemed to be much more interested in you and whatever you and I had been discussing."

Wesley suppressed a sigh. He was getting nowhere. He could not fathom how he had gotten so off course that evening. He'd had no intention of confronting Lady Anne, and then once he had, he was bewildered how the conversation had gotten so off course. He had been unable to hold onto his justifiable anger at the young woman. It was as though she had cast a spell over him, he thought rather dazedly. She would bear watching, he determined.

He could almost feel her discomfort as she valiantly met his eyes. Wesley forced himself to ignore the shaft of guilt that speared through him as he attempted to fan the flames of his anger toward her. He watched in fascination as her blue eyes widened as she continued to meet his glare. For a brief moment her gaze dropped from his, but then it swept back and her pointy little chin lifted in a slight but defiant tilt. Once again, Wesley had to fight not to laugh over the imagery of a kitten standing up to the guard dog that flashed through his mind at her refusal to cower before him.

It was blatantly obvious to him how difficult it was for her to stand her ground. She was doing so in an understated way that many might not even notice, but he could see it. And he found it surprisingly, profoundly attractive. He shoved the unwelcome thought from his mind and scowled at her.

~~~

Anne felt the colour ebb and flow from her cheeks. Her nerves made her almost light headed, and she could not understand why she was fighting him. Of course, other women would probably fight harder or louder. But for her, this was a fight. And it made absolutely no sense to her. *Why should I fight the Viscount of Bracondale?* she wondered almost wildly. In that moment she decided to give up. There was no logical sense to the strange situation.

She was in London to find a husband. It was as simple as that. She did not want a husband who glared at her for something she did not do. So the viscount was not on the list of potential mates. So this thing, whatever it was, that was happening this evening was an unwelcome distraction on her path to a secure future.

Her resolve firmly bolstered, Anne plastered a serene expression upon her face and offered the viscount a tentative smile. A part of her felt like giggling over the suspicious look that crossed the nobleman's face, but she quickly squashed the ridiculous notion. She silently offered up a prayer that the dance would soon be over.

Profound relief spread over her as she heard the music drawing to a conclusion. Just as she was wondering how to dismiss the viscount, she spotted her aunt waiting for her on the side of the dance floor.
~~~

"Thank you for the dance, my lord. I can see that my aunt is looking for me. Perhaps it is time for us to depart."

"Allow me to escort you to her side." His haughty tone set her teeth on edge, but she merely offered him a benign smile.

Anne wondered if she needed to introduce the viscount to her aunt. It seemed to her that the members of the *ton* all knew each other in some mysterious way, but it was proper to perform introductions none the less. She was relieved from this one worry when the viscount bowed elegantly over her aunt's hand.

"My dear Lady Sophie, it is a pleasure to see you again. You look to be in fine health and looking lovely as always this evening. And how is your husband?"

"Oh my lord, you are such a flatterer, you young scamp. We are both well, thank you for asking. We are having a grand time escorting my niece around the events of the Season. How lovely that the two of you have met."

Anne could hardly believe it. Her usually prosaic aunt was practically simpering over the viscount's attentions. Her jaw nearly became unhinged over the viscount's next words.

"It has been my pleasure meeting your niece. In fact, I was wondering if I might have the pleasure of escorting her for the promenade in the Park tomorrow afternoon."

A buzzing began in her ears, and Anne almost missed her aunt's reply. Of course, the delight plastered all over her face was really answer enough, Anne thought while fighting a fit of hysterics. *What is the viscount up to?* she wondered frantically as she used every ounce of her willpower to maintain her composure.

She was in a bewildered haze as she watched his retreating back for a brief moment. Not wanting to appear as a love struck sot, she turned her attention back to her aunt. She regretted that choice as soon as her aunt opened her mouth.

"How very exciting, my dear. The Viscount of Bracondale! You could do far worse than him. If the rumours are true, his coffers are so deep even your father wouldn't be able to run through them in what is left of his lifetime."

Anne had no reply for such a statement. Her throat spasmed painfully as she struggled to contain her feelings of revulsion.

Anne's aunt didn't seem to notice that Anne did not appear overjoyed at the prospect of entertaining a visit with the viscount on the morrow. "This is perfect, my dear. The Viscount of Bracondale." She repeated his name again as though it were an invocation.

Anne's stomach turned, and she wondered miserably how much longer it would be before she could seek her bed. As though she had read her niece's mind, her aunt finally looked at her.

"You look a trifle piqued, my dear. I think we ought to get you home to bed. It would not do to be overly tired for your ride with the viscount tomorrow. Come along, my dear. I shall have a footman fetch your uncle and have the carriage called for. Let us go and take our leave of our hostess."

Anne followed dully in her aunt's wake as she wondered how her life had gotten so dreadfully off course.

Chapter Two

Anne awakened to a dull headache. She'd had difficulty falling asleep the night before as she worried about her encounter with the viscount. *What did the man want with her?* she wondered for the hundredth time. Determined not to waste another minute of worry, she shoved back the covers and swung her legs over the side of the bed as her maid drew the drapes.

Accepting her morning cup of chocolate from her maid, Anne acknowledged that life in her aunt's household was decidedly better than on her father's estate in many ways. There were far fewer drafts here, for one thing. And for another, there were enough servants that one could actually be given the task of bringing her such a delicious, warm treat every morning. Anne allowed a contented sigh to escape her lips as she indulged in the decadent delight of being pampered.

Then she gave her head a shake. She ought not to grow accustomed to such comforts. She was beginning to suspect that she would have to return to their rundown estate with her father when this Season was over. If word got out about what she had almost done for her father and his friend, no one would want to take her as his wife. And even if word did not get out, she wasn't sure if she would be able to trust her own judgment or trust that her father was not somehow being manipulated into manipulating her by one of his twisted and wicked friends.

She thought back over the night before. The viscount had good reason to be furious with her. She knew she was not the brightest young woman, but she should have realized there was something havey-cavey about her father encouraging her to set her cap for the Duke of Wrentham. Anne shuddered at the thought of what would have happened if that plan had not been averted. She did not expect a love match, but the thought of being married to someone who resented her for tricking him filled her with dread. *Perhaps it would be better to remain unmarried*, she thought with a lack of conviction. It would no doubt be better for her peace of mind, on the one hand. But knowing that her father was counting on her to pull them out of the suds did not bode well for any possible peace of mind.

Perhaps she could discuss the entire quandary with her aunt. That cheering thought bolstered her lagging spirits, and she stepped down from the bed and allowed the attentive maid to fuss with her hair and get her gowned.

Anne fingered the beautiful gown while the maid did the myriad buttons up the back. It had been years since she had worn such fine fabrics. While it wasn't until her mother died that her father had lost all control of their finances, even while she was still alive they had not had an overabundance of spending money. Anne hated to think about it, but she suspected lack of funds might have contributed to her mother's quick decline into the grave.

It was unlike her to be so melancholy. She tried to shake the negative thoughts. Anne knew her father counted on her to be steady, without highs and lows of emotion. It wasn't always easy. She had feelings just like everyone, but she did try to keep them under wraps to the best of her ability. It really helped if she didn't think too hard about any one thing. But ever since her father told her what had been behind his suggestion that she set her cap for the duke, she had been having a difficult time restricting her thoughts. She had been filled with such anger, which was a foreign experience for her. But her father claimed to love her. How could he have thought it would be all right to arrange for her to marry someone so his friend could control her new husband for some sort of nefarious purpose? It was not to be borne.

Unfortunately, this line of thought was putting her out of sorts. Her father had not appreciated her thoughts on the matter when she told him how she felt. She rather suspected he was ashamed of the situation and didn't know how to face her. Anne hadn't seen her father for two days now. She hoped he had perhaps returned the evening before.

That thought spurred her to hurry into the breakfast room, but it was empty save for the footman waiting patiently for the last of the family members to break their fast.

"Good morning, my lady," the footman called out cheerfully.

"Good morning, Jason," she replied, trying to infuse some warmth into her voice. It was not the servant's fault she was disappointed.

Glancing at the clock on the mantle, Anne was surprised to see how much of the day had already passed. "Gracious! Am I the last one up this morning?"

"I do believe so, my lady."

"I apologize if I have made you late for your other duties."

"Pay it no mind, my lady."

Anne was embarrassed to have kept the footman waiting even though she was well aware it was part of his job. She had grown accustomed to looking after herself these past few years and while it was pleasant to have servants to do things for her, she had a guilty feeling that it wasn't quite right to be waited on. She knew other members of the *ton* would decry her bourgeois sentiments, but Anne couldn't quite decide exactly how she felt on the subject.

"Are you aware if my father has returned?"

"I am not aware, my lady. Would you like me to go ask the butler for you?"

Anne bit her lip, wondering what the proper course of action would be. Caving in to her intense desire to know her father's whereabouts, she accepted the servant's offer.

"Thank you, Jason, I would appreciate that."

The footman waited until she had filled her plate and was seated before he left the room. Anne managed not to fidget too much and picked at the food on her plate while she awaited his return. Thankfully, she was not left waiting too long.

"I'm sorry, my lady, your father hasn't been seen."

The mouthful she had been chewing suddenly tasted like sand as her mouth went dry. She was really getting nervous about his absence and had no one with whom to talk the matter over. Anne had recently become aware that her father had unsavoury associates. She made an effort to contain her anxiety, but her appetite was well and truly gone. With regret, she pushed aside her plate and got to her feet.

"Have you seen my aunt this morning, Jason?"

"Yes, my lady, I believe she is working on her correspondence in the morning room."

"Thank you, Jason." Anne quickly left the room, fighting her guilt over the wasted food. Chastising herself for being a ninny, she reminded herself once more that while she was in her aunt's house, she was not the impoverished innocent she had been before arriving in London.

Moving as quickly but as gracefully as she could manage, Anne arrived in her aunt's morning room only moments later. She paused at the door watching, as the older woman appeared deep in thought. Aunt Sophie was older than her mother would have been. All her children were already grown and married, which is why, Anne supposed, she had been willing to take her and her Season on. She felt a warm fondness as she gazed at the older woman.

"Good morning, my lady, do you have a minute?"

"For you, my darling girl? Always! And please, you must call me Aunt Sophie." Lady Sophie bustled around putting away her correspondence as she prattled on. "It is deplorable that we never knew each other better than we do. I really should have kept in better touch with my poor dear sister. You will never know how much I regret that, my dear. But I am hoping to make up for lost time. Come, have a seat. What did you want to talk about? Is it about that charming viscount who is coming to take you for a ride this afternoon?"

Anne stifled her groan. She had wanted to pour out her worries, but her aunt's prattle made her question whether she could bear to hear about her worries. Anne decided to keep her thoughts to herself for a while longer.

"I really don't think Lord Dunbar has any sort of marital intentions toward me, my lady, I mean Aunt Sophie. I do hope you don't get your hopes up too high."

Lady Sophie laughed over her niece's words. "My dear, you sound like the old matron, and I sound like the debutante in this conversation. Why are you not more excited about the prospect of riding out with him this afternoon? Is there something wrong with the gentleman? He is very well reported on, I must tell you. And reputed to be remarkably wealthy. Would you like me to have your uncle look into him, if there is something in particular you are concerned about?"

Her aunt's deluge of questions caused Anne to be even more reluctant to share her thoughts on the subject. "No, no, nothing like that. I am sure he is perfectly lovely and above board. It is just that when I was dancing with him, I did not at all get the impression that he has any serious thought of getting a wife for himself any time soon. I think he offered to take me for a drive more out of a desire to turn you up sweet than to fix his interests with me."

This observation caused Lady Sophie to let out a hoot of laughter. "Why would the poor boy want to turn me up sweet?"

"Perhaps he is after your husband for some political influence. Lord Dunbar's friend told me last night that he only attends balls for that very reason."

"I can assure you, my dear, any gentleman who takes a look at you isn't thinking about advancing his political career."

Anne knew her aunt meant it as a compliment, but she had a mirror in her room and she was quite well aware that she was far from a diamond. And she barely had a dowry, so there was very little to recommend her as a potential bride. She stifled the sigh wanting to escape. Not wanting to concern her aunt, she turned the subject.

"I actually wanted to ask you if you had any idea how we might find my father. I haven't heard from him in two days and am beginning to get concerned."

A change came over Lady Sophie's features at this. "I do not wish to speak ill of your father, my dear, but his absence would not do your prospects any harm. In fact, I am thinking that he probably finally took your uncle's suggestion that he clear out completely until we get you settled."

Anne felt the blood draining from her face at her aunt's words. "But surely he wouldn't just leave without even saying goodbye," she cried. While she was angry with him over his manipulative ways, he was still the only family she had left. Her aunt was lovely, but Anne still felt as though she were practically a stranger. "I know my father has many faults, but he is still my father, and I am quite certain he would not just clear out without a word. Would it be possible for me to talk to my uncle about this? Might he have someone we could set upon looking for my father?"

Lady Sophie sniffed disdainfully but then relented. "You are no doubt right, my dear. We shall talk to your uncle about it, but I doubt he has any notion how to find him either."

Anne stifled a sigh. She should have known better than to bring it up. It wasn't as though her aunt had made any effort to hide the disdain she felt for Lord Austen. There was little to wonder about that her mother had kept communication to a minimum with her family if that was how they felt about her husband. Anne was well aware that her father had some glaring flaws, but he had been a loving father and husband while his wife had been alive.

Forcing a smile to her face, Anne got to her feet. She tried to be nonchalant as she wandered about the room, trying to delicately take her leave of her aunt. She would have to work out her disturbed feelings on her own, she realized.

"Thank you for taking the time to speak with me. I ought to go and write some letters of my own. And then, of course, I have to get ready for my drive. Perhaps I will take a little nap before the viscount arrives in order to ensure I have the energy for this evening as well."

"That as a brilliant idea, my dear. It wouldn't do to be looking less than your best."

Anne kept a smile on her face while she fought not to roll her eyes. She wished she could talk to one of her new friends. It was their influence that had brought about this urge to think for herself. She knew she ought to be upset about this change, as it was complicating her life, but she couldn't help but be proud of herself for trying to take control of herself.

"Not that it will do much good," she grumbled as she entered her room.

"What's that, my lady?" the maid questioned with a furrowed brow.

Anne started and felt an embarrassed blush rising in her cheeks. "Oh, I was just talking to myself, please, pay it no mind."

The maid bobbed a curtsy and continued with her work, but Anne could feel her watching her out of the corner of her eye. There was something to be said for having barely any servants, she thought. At least one could manage a few moments alone. Regretting her uncharitable thoughts, Anne smiled at the maid despite the fact that she was pretending not to watch her.

Miraculously the day passed quickly while Anne brooded over her options. Before she knew it, the moment she was dreading arrived. The footman knocked at her door and informed her the viscount was waiting for her.

Anne grabbed her gloves, glanced in the mirror to ensure all the buttons on her spencer were done up straight, and was gratified to see that her turmoil was not visible. Even her hair was behaving itself beautifully today. With a fanciful grimace at herself, she noted that if she believed in fate she would be much more excited about this outing. As it was, she had to force her feet toward the stairs.

Lady Sophie was enthusiastically entertaining Lord Dunbar as he waited for her. Anne paused at the door to observe his air of patient kindness as her aunt regaled him with some piece of gossip that she had gleaned from her cronies the night before.

"How very interesting," he murmured politely before he caught sight of Anne hovering by the door. "Good day to you, Lady Anne. You look charming on this fine afternoon." He paused for a moment before continuing. "It is the strangest thing, my lady. It seems to be that you grow more lovely each time I see you."

Anne couldn't help it, she rolled her eyes and laughed at his words. "Are you in your cups, my lord?"

Her words surprised a chuckle out of the viscount, but all he said in answer was, "Not at all, my dear. Shall we depart?"

Hoping her hand wouldn't tremble and reveal her agitated feelings, Anne allowed the viscount to pull it through his elbow as he escorted her to his waiting carriage.

"There's no need for you to rush back, Anne, my dear. We are not promised anywhere overly early this evening."

Anne was embarrassed at her aunt's words. There was no call to be so blatant, she thought with vehemence. It took her several moments before she could face the viscount while she battled her intense mortification. When she finally could look at him, she was relieved to see that he appeared not to have even noticed. No doubt it was a regular occurrence, she realized. This thought both cheered her and depressed her all at once. She resolved not to think about it.

Realizing the silence was stretching a little thin, Anne strove for an innocuous topic to discuss. "It's a lovely day for a drive," she offered, happy to hear that her voice was steady even if it was rather subdued.

~~~

Wesley glanced at his companion, the mixture of feelings he experienced while in her presence was almost becoming familiar. He was angry and suspicious of her intentions, and yet he felt the need to protect her. From what, he would not be able to tell you. Her voice, although almost timid, was melodious and had a disconcerting effect upon him. He felt as though he could listen to her all day, even if it were just inane pleasantries about the weather.

Determined to have a proper conversation with her, Wesley shoved the unwelcome thoughts aside for the moment and hoped he could get her to talk. "That it is, my lady. Thank you for accompanying me."

He was surprised to see a twinkle in her eye as she asked him, in a prim voice, "What would you have done if I had refused? It isn't as though you even asked me. You asked my aunt instead. I was of a mind to tell her to accompany you herself."

Wesley couldn't help laughing over her words. "Well, that would have certainly taught me a lesson, wouldn't it?" He was glad to see she was in on the joke and not taking offense over his laughter. "I apologize, my lady, if I was overbearing."

"No need to apologize, my lord. I am quite well aware that is how things are done. It just doesn't strike me as being terribly polite. I am a person, too. It is disconcerting to be discussed as though I haven't a mind of my own."

Feeling his eyebrows rising over her words, Wesley tried to keep his tone even as he replied. "Do you, my lady? You have given the impression of being an obedient girl who follows her father's wishes."
~~~

He fought his fascination as her colour rose. She couldn't meet his eyes, but her chin rose in a display of defiance. "Recent events have helped me to see that a different approach might benefit me."

"Really?" Wesley wished he did not have to concentrate on his horses as they passed through a busy section of road. He wanted to delve deeper into her statement and watch her face closely as they talked. He quickly resolved that they ought to walk as soon as they got to the Park.

Anne did not reply to his one-word question, and Wesley allowed the silence to return as he guided his well-matched bays through the entrance into the Park. They were a little early for the truly fashionable hour, which was perfect for his plans to get her to talk.

"How would you feel about taking a stroll first? We could drive around later when it gets a bit busier here."

Anne cocked her head curiously. "Would it not make more sense to drive now and walk later? Isn't it irritating to try to drive around when the pathways get crowded?"

Again, Wesley had to laugh over her words. "Well, yes, it is irritating, but it is what one does during the Season. Do you not want to see and be seen?"

He almost missed her muttered, "Not really," and wondered at her contradictory behaviour. She still hadn't answered his question, and Wesley's patience was wearing thin. He wanted answers from this young woman. He pulled his team over to the side of the road and was glad when his tiger jumped down quickly to take their leads. He knew the high strung horses would be in good hands with his young servant.

Wesley felt Anne watching him intently. He reached up and lifted her down from the high carriage. "Come along, my lady. We shall be much more comfortable this way."

Her dubious expression revealed that she doubted his statement, but she did not object as he set her on her feet. The viscount was again unnerved by her petite presence. His continued anger with her vied with a desire to protect her, even if it was from himself. He hoped she was unaware of either of his sentiments. Her downcast eyes revealed nothing of her thoughts.

They walked down a path that was less populated than the main thoroughfare. It was still perfectly respectable, but would allow them a level of privacy for the discussion he wished to have. He couldn't think of any delicate way to lead up to the main point, so he just plunged in.

"Does your newfound desire for thoughts of your own have anything to do with your father's scheme to entrap the Duke of Wrentham?"

Wesley could tell his question had caught her off guard by the way she stiffened slightly at his side, but anyone watching them would be hard pressed to tell that anything was amiss. She barely revealed by the flicker of an eyelash that his question had discomfited her.

"Why do you ask, my lord?" she countered.

"Because I am furious with you for your efforts to entrap my friend, and I would like to know if there are any other schemes afoot." Wesley answered her honestly but tried to control the fury that was creeping into his voice.

He couldn't believe it when a tinkle of laughter escaped his companion. He didn't want to draw undue attention to them, but he couldn't help stopping dead in his tracks. "How can you find this amusing?" he demanded.

"I apologize, my lord, you are quite correct. There is nothing amusing about this situation, aside from the fact that my aunt was quite convinced that you were displaying a marked interest in me and was delighted at the prospect. I laughed when I thought about how sadly mistaken she was. I had tried to convince her that she could not be accurate in her assumptions, but she was steadfast in her thoughts. It is always gratifying to know that one was right, even if it is an uncomfortable topic."

Wesley couldn't believe what he was hearing. "Your aunt thought I was trying to court you?" he was incredulous.

Anne shrugged. "You did invite me to go for a drive in the Park during the fashionable hour. It is a common practice when a gentleman is trying to fix a lady's interest, my lord."

Wesley felt heat gathering in his cheeks. "You are right. I apologize, my lady. But why did you not follow along with your aunt's line of thought?"

Anne pierced him with her perceptive gaze. "While you have been making every attempt to be civilized about it, my lord, it is obvious that you are angry with me. In fact, you have even told me so. It is not the usual frame of mind for a courting gentleman."

He had to grin over her words. "I am sure you are correct, my lady." Now he was curious. "Have you had many men courting you this Season?"

Again the lady shrugged. "No." There was a pause while she avoided any eye contact. "My dowry is negligible, my father is a known spendthrift, and my family connections are not stellar. It was doubtful that I would make a brilliant match when we first arrived. Now, if my share in my father's scheme becomes known, no match will be likely."

"You don't seem overly troubled by this." Wesley was perplexed over the lady's reaction. And he was beginning to find her repeated negligent shrugs to be irritating. He was surprised when she finally met his gaze with her own bright blue one.

"I am personally rather confused with how I feel on the entire subject, my lord. And unfortunately, I have no one to discuss the matter with."

Wesley blanched over her words. He was so conflicted about this young woman. As a gentleman, he could not leave a lady in distress; it was just one more layer to the awkward situation. He surprised himself with his next words.

"Since I am already involved in the situation, perhaps you could discuss it with me."

He fully understood the shock reflected in her gaze. "But you are angry with me, my lord. I doubt you will be the most objective listener on the subject."

"Actually, if we talk about it, it might help me be less angry as I come to understand your perspective on the matter."

There was a moment of taut silence while she appeared to mull the matter over. The viscount was taken aback by the sensation of relief that swept through him when she nodded.

~~~

Anne could hardly believe she was going to take the viscount up on his unorthodox offer. But she had no one to turn to and was feeling desperate to talk to someone. She took a deep breath and plunged in.

"I don't even know where to start, my lord. I was furious with my father when I found out what was behind his encouraging me to set my cap at the duke. Whether you believe me or not, I had no intention of trying to help Sir Broderick. I find that odious man to be repulsive."

"Why, Lady Anne, that is the most vehement statement I have ever heard you make."

Anne was surprised by the viscount's teasing tone. Bashful, she answered him. "Do you not agree with my sentiments, though, my lord? I do not understand how the man is accepted everywhere! He puts me in mind of something one might find under a rock."

Wesley chuckled. "Very well, my lady, I find that I am becoming convinced that you were not complicit in Broderick's scheme. But then, why would you agree to your father's suggestion that you try to entrap the duke into making you an offer?"

Anne was swept with a wave of mortification. She suddenly realized how awkward this conversation was going to become. Grimly, she acknowledged that she strongly doubted the viscount would divulge the details of their conversation. And since he was not actually interested in her for matrimony, she
~~~

had little to lose by telling him the truth. And it would be such a relief to discuss the matter with someone.

She looked the viscount in the eye, somewhat exasperated by the dense question. "Really, my lord? Do you have to ask? Look at me. My chances of getting married this Season are slim. I am not a great beauty, I have no wealth or family to recommend me. It seemed like an expedient way to make a brilliant match. I allowed myself to be swept up in the idea that being a duchess would be lovely." She paused her words for a moment as they continued walking slowly. Then she turned to Lord Dunbar. "To be honest, I didn't give it a whole lot of thought. I was in the habit of following the direction given to me without questioning it. I have not been in the habit of having independent thoughts. When my father suggested what he thought was a brilliant idea, I went along with it. It wasn't until Lady Elizabeth and Miss Smythe discussed it with me that I even considered an alternative. And then when I finally found out what my father's intentions had been, I was finally motivated to try to think things through for myself."

"Have you come to any conclusions?" the viscount asked quietly.

Anne could hear that her small laugh was tinged with bitterness. "Not really, regretfully." She sighed before continuing. "If I had any means of achieving it, I would wish to establish my own home and never need to be dependent on a man ever again. But my father is depending on me to marry someone with the financial ability to save us from penury. I am beginning to feel that the idea is repugnant."

"But it is a common enough motivation behind many of the marriages of the *ton*," the viscount pointed out reasonably.

"Perhaps so, but who is going to want me? As I stated before, there is very little to recommend a match with me." Anne wasn't fishing for compliments. She genuinely felt hopeless on the subject.

Chapter Three

Wesley was again swept with a strong desire to protect the young woman at his side. His anger towards her was sufficiently squelched. He could see how she might have gotten entangled in the scheme without realizing what was involved, and so he determined to help her.

"My friends and I could help you."

"How, my lord? Are you planning to offer for me after all?"

Wesley could tell from her tone of voice that she thought the idea was ridiculous. Shockingly, he didn't fully agree with her. But he had no interest in giving up his unwedded state any time soon. He appreciated her being honest with him, so he gave her the same courtesy.

"I have no desire to get leg shackled at this time, my lady, but I do believe the duke would expect me to help you out, despite your involvement with his enemies. He is very happy with how things have worked out after all and is feeling decidedly magnanimous. I know he would consider it his obligation as a gentleman to ensure that no scandal attaches itself to you. Since he is not here to see to that himself, I will do so in his stead."

"What exactly do you have in mind, my lord? I am uncertain if I am comfortable with you trying to sort out my life for me."

"I promise you I shan't do anything you do not agree to. I was merely thinking that my friends and I could pay you some attention. This would draw other gentlemen's attention. Before you know it, you will have to pick between multiple offers."

Wesley felt a warm tendril unfurl within his chest when he heard her rich chuckle. "You, my lord, are a devious one, aren't you? Do you really think you have that much influence over other members of the *ton*?"

"I hate to sound like an arrogant dunce, but yes, I do believe it would be easy enough to do. Most people are followers. If it was just me paying attention to you, some might dismiss it. But if I get my friends involved, it will surely take effect."

"I thought you hate schemes." Wesley heard the suspicion in her voice.

"When they are designed to hurt someone I care about, I do. But in this case, it's for a good cause. Do you intend to be a good and faithful wife if and when we get you matched up with someone?"

"Of course," she stammered, still seeming confused. "But why would your friends agree to such a plan?"

"For any number of reasons, my lady, you need not trouble yourself about that. They will consider it to be a lark, I am sure."

There was a moment of silence while Lady Anne stared straight ahead, deep in thought. "I mean no offense, my lord, but I have to tell you that I feel quite questionable about your motives. But if you really do manage to set such a plan in motion, I can see that it just might work." She gave a helpless sounding laugh that plucked at Wesley's sympathies. "Unfortunately, my wish for a life of independence is highly impractical. If you could manage to find me an appropriate gentleman to wed, I would be most grateful."

Wesley ignored the impulse he felt to withdraw his offer. His word as a gentleman was his bond. The sooner he could get the chit attached to someone, the better it would be for his peace of mind. She was nothing but trouble.

"Do you know which entertainments your aunt is planning to take you to this evening?"

"Not entirely, my lord. I must admit that I haven't been paying very close attention to these matters over the past couple of days. She did mention, as we were leaving, that we didn't have to be anywhere too early, so I would think that means we are not attending any dinner parties. I am fairly certain we accepted an invitation to a ball at Clairhurst for this evening. I'm sorry. I am not very helpful, am I?"

"Don't go backsliding into mousy behaviour now, my dear. You have been shoring up your gumption for a couple of days. Pay it no mind for now. Find out what you can about your future engagements. We will track you down this evening and set our plans in motion."

He felt his protective urges stirring once more as Lady Anne grabbed his arm and turned her luminous eyes toward him. He could feel it as though it were a tangible thing as she chose to put her trust in him. "Thank you, my lord. I know I don't deserve your assistance in this matter, but I am deeply grateful for it none the less. I will do my best to be cooperative.

Patting her hand and feeling uncomfortable with her gratitude, Wesley strove for a change of topic as he turned and headed back with her toward his carriage. "I didn't notice your father at the ball last night nor again today when I arrived at your aunt's house. Previously it seemed as though he was always hovering around you protectively."

Again, her eyes slid nervously away from his gaze, and Wesley felt his suspicions rising. But then she quickly turned her eyes to meet his, and he could see tears welling in them.

"Oh, my lord, I do not know what has become of him. He hasn't been seen for a couple of days, ever since he told me why he wanted me to set my cap for the duke. I was incensed with him for the first time in my life, and I said a couple things I probably shouldn't have. He stormed out and, as far as I know, he hasn't come back. It is another thing I am worrying about, to be honest. My aunt thinks he has probably just taken off in order not to spoil my chances, but I really don't think he would have gone back home without saying goodbye to me."

Wesley found himself rubbing her hand as it lay on his arm, trying to offer what little comfort he could. He fought an irrational desire to put his arm around her and still the trembling he could feel from her. "What do you think could have happened to him? Is it really that far out of his character?"

Anne shook her head. "I have no idea where he might be. Until my mother died, he was the steadiest character you would ever encounter. Since then, I keep telling myself that nothing he does should surprise me. But I know he cares about me and would not want me to fret. I worry that his unsavoury companions have done him harm."

She returned her tear-filled gaze to his once more, and Wesley felt his chest tighten. "Do not work yourself up into a taking, my lady. I tell you what. I will set a Runner onto the case. I am sure he has just done as your aunt said. He is probably squirreled away on his estate."

"Would you really send someone to look for him?" Wesley felt as though he were taller as the young woman looked at him so admiringly. "I hate for you to go to such an expense on my account, my lord, but oh, I would so appreciate it."

"Never mind about the expense, my dear, it actually costs woefully little to hire a Runner. They really ought to value themselves higher. Now come along. Let me drive you through the Park as I promised and then I must see you home. If I am to set this plan in motion, I need to meet with my friends before the evening."

~~~

Anne quickened her pace, trying to keep up with Wesley's suddenly lengthening stride. She was feeling overwhelmed with all the sudden changes. Who would have ever thought that she
~~~

would be feeling so friendly towards the Viscount of Bracondale? Or that he would appear to want to stand by her as a friend. She knew she had no real reason to trust the nobleman, but he really did inspire confidence in her. For the first time since she had arrived in London, she was feeling optimistic about her chances of making an advantageous match. And if a little piece of her heart fluttered a trifle too energetically while in the vicinity of the viscount, that was just going to be her own trial to bear. He must never know about it.

When they arrived back at the viscount's phaeton, he lifted her into it as though she weighed a feather, which sent another thrill through Anne, one that she once more chose to ignore. Once the viscount gained his seat, they rolled out, taking their place in the slow queue of vehicles circling the Park. He was a skilled driver and made quick work of manoeuvring through the congestion. They took a turn around the Park then headed back toward Anne's temporary dwelling.

She was grateful for the idle chatter the viscount kept up as he tooled her around in his phaeton. Anne began to relax and actually enjoy the outing. She chuckled over his wry comments about others in the Park that day, despite casting him a reproving glance.

"My lord, you really ought not to fill my head with such opinions. I cannot say for sure if I can be trusted not to blurt them out at the most inappropriate times."

"Are you planning to change into a different person over night?" he asked, surprise evident in his voice.

"No, why?" she queried.

"It seems to me that you never speak without thinking it through rather thoroughly."

Anne had to laugh over his words. "I wish that was the case, my lord. No, I have not been recently in the habit of thinking much at all, I am afraid. It is a painful thing to realize and acknowledge about myself. But I think I have been unforgivably foolish."

"Not unforgivably, surely, my lady." Wesley's tone was back to teasing, and Anne was forced to laugh despite her discomfort.

"Well, never mind, I have every intention of changing that now. But I suppose you are correct in that I am not really a blurter. I should think your statements are safe with me. You really are terribly droll, though, I must say, my lord."

"I do aim to please, my lady."

"I didn't say I was pleased, my lord, merely that I was amused." She would rather die than let the viscount know he made her feel fluttery. It was a ridiculous situation.

"Thank you for the drive, Lord Dunbar. I appreciate the attention you are giving to my troubles. I will make every effort not to be more of a burden than necessary." Anne said this as the viscount was lifting her down once more.

His reply, said over her shoulder just as he put her on her feet, sent another thrill along her nerve endings. "A lady could never be considered a burden, Lady Anne." She knew he was merely being gallant and she ought to dismiss his words as the nonsense they were, but Anne could not help it when her heart picked up its pace within her chest. She didn't bother replying, as she couldn't for the life of her come up with anything to say.

After the footman opened the door to her, Anne greeted him politely and then ran up to her room. Leaning her back against the door, she gazed at the ceiling, thinking over the ups and downs the day had taken. She didn't know if the viscount's plan would work, but she couldn't help feeling much more positive about her prospects for the future. With a grin, she summoned her maid to begin her preparations for the evening.

~~~

Wesley drove around to his club, not overly far from where he had dropped off Anne, certain the gentlemen he was looking for would be gathered there. It had become their custom most afternoons to meet up and have a brief visit, checking in with one another.
~~~

He pondered how best to broach the subject with his friends but realized only the truth would do. Jumping down from his phaeton, he bade his servant to take his team home. He would just as rather walk home after meeting with his friends.

Sure enough, when he stepped into the club, he was greeted cheerfully by an attentive footman. "Good afternoon, my lord, we had just about given up on you coming this afternoon. Your friends have nearly finished off their decanter without you."

"That is excellent news. They should be in receptive spirits then." Wesley grinned. "Are any of the private rooms available just now?"

"Of course, I can show you to one immediately."

"Let us pass by my friends on the way. I was hoping they would join me."

"Very well, my lord." The footman bowed and carried on, leading the way to where Lord Grey and Lord Sutton were seated.

"Dunbar!" Sebastian Grey exclaimed, delight evident in his wide grin. "We had quite given you up for today. Where have you been hiding yourself?"

"I was out for a drive," Wesley replied, grasping his friend's outstretched hand in a firm handshake. "It is partially that which I would like to discuss with the two of you, if you would be so good as to accompany me where we could have a bit of privacy."

The earl rose slowly to his feet, very much the more sardonic of the trio. "What kind of trouble are you about to get us into Dunbar?" His drawl was belied by the twinkle Wesley could see shining in his eye. James Grant Spencer, the Fifth Earl of Sutton, was always ready to jump in when his friends needed him.

The two friends must have noticed how serious Wesley appeared because they quit their good-natured teasing and followed where the viscount led. The footman ushered them into a small book room, set down a bottle of brandy and some glasses, and then left them, silently closing the door on his way out.

As soon as the door closed behind the servant, Lord Grey burst out, "What is going on, Dunbar? It's unusual for you to be able to contain yourself with a secret. Is this more of Wrentham's mess? The two of you left us out in the cold up until now." The nobleman scoffed. "What happened? Did you realize you cannot do it on your own?"

"In a manner of speaking, yes," Wesley replied softly, bringing the sharp gazes of his friends swiftly to meet his own. All the teasing went out of their faces, and the atmosphere in the room became quite serious.

"Out with it, Dunbar, you know we are at your service," the earl stated with quiet dignity.

Wesley broke the stiff silence by grinning at his friends. "I am absolutely confident that I can rely on you. That is why we are here. And yes, it is somewhat related to that other matter. Have you been drinking all afternoon? I need to fortify myself before I launch into the tale."

They each held out their glass for Wesley to fill. Once they had all tossed back their drinks, Wesley started in on his explanation.

"Remember how I told you that a young lady was planning to entrap Alex into marriage in order for that swine Broderick to gain access to his influence?"

"I remember thinking it was a daft plan, but yes, it was just last week, so we definitely recall your story. Go on."

Wesley didn't bother disputing with the earl over it. It was old news now, so he got to his point. "Well, I need your assistance in helping that young lady."

"Helping her with what?" Sebastian demanded. "And why in the name of all that's holy would we offer her any sort of assistance? Do you not recall that you just told us she was trying to entrap our brother?"

"She appears to have seen the error of her ways. In fact, I no longer believe she ever meant him harm. She wasn't in league with Broderick's schemes. She merely sought a well-healed husband, a normal enough pursuit amongst ladies of the *ton*. Besides, you know Wrentham would want us to help her."

"But he's soft as a kitten most of the time," Sebastian scoffed. "And more to the point, he's not here."

"Exactly. He's not here, so he would expect us to do this for him in his absence."

The earl had been watching this exchange with cold perception. "Have you gone soft on us now, too, Dunbar? Or did the wench turn you up sweet?"

Wesley knew his cheeks were growing warm but chose to ignore it and brazened it out. "Neither," he declared with resolution. "It was my idea. If word gets out about her involvement, she'll be ruined."

"And well she should be," Sebastian spluttered, still disbelieving their friend would want them to help someone he clearly viewed as an enemy.

Always the steadier of the crew, the earl continued to watch Wesley. "What exactly did you have in mind? I danced with her last night. She seems to be reasonable enough, for a female, but I really doubt you are going to expect one of us to make an offer for the chit, so how can we help her out?"

"If all three of us start to show an interest in her, it will cause a stir and get other gentlemen interested. Before too long she'll have a couple offers to choose from, and she will be off our hands."

Sutton continued to watch Wesley, and the viscount held his gaze. "Very well, it sounds like a reasonably simple plan. When did you want to start?"

Wesley could barely believe it had been that easy. Sebastian blustered a little longer but within moments the three had agreed to meet at the Clairhurst ball that evening in order to put their plan into action.

"Is she a complete dowd?" Sebastian thought to ask, just before they took leave of one another.

"Why would you ask that?" Wesley asked, puzzled.

Sebastian eyed the viscount, obviously perplexed that he would question the obvious. "She would not need our help finding a husband otherwise, would she?"

Wesley chuckled over his friend's comment. "I can see why you would say so, but no. While she is a trifle mousy, I would not say she is a dowd." He paused in thought and then shrugged. "You shall see for yourself this evening," he finally concluded.

Sutton's amused gaze watching him irritated Wesley. He recalled Anne's words about the earl. Wesley wondered what the other man was thinking but decided he didn't really want to know. They had agreed to a course of action, it wasn't the time for second guessing.

Within minutes the decanter was empty and the three gentlemen took their leave of one another after finalizing their arrangements to meet at the Clairhurst ball.

Chapter Four

Anne felt as though a swarm of butterflies had taken up residence in her inward parts. She was so nervous about the upcoming evening she could barely sit still while the maid arranged her hair.

"What has gotten into you, milady?" Sally demanded, clearly impatient with her mistress's uncharacteristic behaviour.

"Oh, do hurry, Sally, please. I am ever so anxious to get going."

"Well, I don't see no sense in hurrying since your aunt won't be ready any faster than usual, milady. Now sit still or your hair will be crooked, and then it'll be me that gets the sack, not you."

Anne subsided. She probably ought not to allow the servant to speak so disrespectfully to her, but she didn't have the heart to reprimand her. She was trying to save all her bravery and gumption for the evening ahead. She wondered if the viscount would really follow through with his offer to help her. It still struck her as odd that he would make any effort to go out of his way to help her when he had been so obviously furious with her before. But she wasn't about to look a gift horse in the mouth. If he did help her, she would be eternally grateful. And for the first time since she had come to London, she was genuinely looking forward to the ball that evening.

She watched as Sally's skilled hands twisted her hair into an intriguing style, transforming her usually nondescript strands into an elegant arrangement. Anne couldn't help admiring her reflection. Her excitement put extra colour into her cheeks, so she was less pale than usual. While she would never be a diamond of the first water, she wasn't going to be the mousiest girl in the room that evening at least.

Finally, the maid finished her ministrations and pronounced her ready for the night. Anne bounded to her feet, thanking the servant swiftly as she ran from the room. She was ready and waiting at the bottom of the stairs before her aunt and uncle made their appearance.

When Lady Sophie saw her niece waiting in the foyer, she exclaimed, "Why, Anne, this is a surprise! You have never seemed so eager to go out before." She smiled coyly at her niece. "Is there something you wish to tell me?"

"Not at all, my lady," Anne answered truthfully, as she had absolutely no desire for her aunt to know what the viscount had offered. "Sally merely managed to get me ready faster than usual, is all."

Anne was a little nervous about how unconvinced Lady Sophie appeared to be, but her uncle quickly changed the subject by clearing his throat. "Never mind about why we're ready when we are, my dear. Should we not just be grateful that we haven't been kept waiting by the girl? I would be just as glad to get on the way. You know how congested the streets are going to be."

"Oh, hush now, husband, do not be disagreeable. Very well, let us be off. I know you though, my lord. You just want to get there so you can get in a few hands of whist before everyone is in their cups."

"Nothing wrong with that, is there?"

The three had a chuckle over this familiar argument as they were handed up into the carriage for the short drive to the Clairhurst ball.

When their carriage finally reached the end of the long line and it was their turn to alight, Anne was struck with an attack of nerves so intense she doubted if she would be able to exit.

She took herself sternly to task. Her and her father's future depended on her getting this right. She squared her shoulders, accepted the footman's outstretched hand, stepped down from the carriage, and followed in her aunt and uncle's wake, all the while praying that her fear was not written all over her features.

Relief spread over her when not a single head turned when they were announced. Previously, her anonymity had caused her great consternation. Now it was a relief. If no one noticed her, it meant no one was talking about her, which meant that scandal had not yet attached itself to her name, and if the viscount stayed true to his promise then she might actually stand a chance of having a decent future. Those were a lot of ifs, she acknowledged, but she wasn't ready to back down just yet.

"Good evening, my lady," Lord Dunbar's voice at her side nearly made her squeak with surprise, as though her thoughts had conjured him. "You are looking lovely."

She almost snorted but just managed not to. It would not do to allow herself to form an exaggerated opinion of herself. That would just be the final straw to make the bad situation worse. But despite those thoughts, she could not help the pink that stained her cheeks or prevent her lashes from sweeping down bashfully. She compressed her lips to prevent them from turning up flirtatiously.

Anne bobbed a curtsy to the viscount but ignored his words. "It is pleasant to see you this evening, my lord." She knew her reply was weak, but she was not yet ready to be effusive. It had only been a day ago that he had been full of fury toward her. She wasn't ready to trust him fully just yet.

The viscount must have been able to read some of the wariness in her bearing because she could see his eyes turn shrewd and assessing before he asked her, "Are you having second thoughts, my lady? Do you wish to call off my plan?"

Her startled gaze flew to meet his. "Not at all, my lord. Why? Are you?" She swallowed the sudden lump of disappointment. "I would understand perfectly if you did, so you needn't be concerned on my behalf." She knew her words were a lie, but it was politeness and self-preservation that motivated her.

"No, you wouldn't," he scoffed, bringing more heat to her cheeks and a reluctant laugh to her lips. "But no, I have not changed my mind. Now, come and dance with me."

Contrarily, his rough words set her at ease, and she happily placed her hand in his as he pulled her into the country dance that was forming. They didn't exchange many words as they moved through the steps, joining and separating, but Anne was content for the first time in what felt like an age, or at least since she and her father had arrived in London. She allowed herself to relax and enjoy the moment while it lasted. Her worries would be waiting for her when it was over.

It was a far cry from the first dance they had shared. Had that just been the night before? Anne wondered in disbelief. It felt as though they were both different people. She certainly felt as though she had changed drastically. And the viscount was definitely acting differently. She still felt a sliver of distrust, but she would allow the moment to be while she merely enjoyed it.

As the dance progressed, she began to feel a prickle of awareness. She gave up on enjoying the moment and allowed her eyes to trail around the room as she circled in the dance. They came to rest on two handsome men standing together next to the dance floor watching her attentively. She must have twitched because the viscount suddenly became alert as well.

"Is aught amiss, my lady?" he asked, his voice low, his head by her ear causing a shiver to run through her, in an attempt not to be overheard.

"Nothing is wrong, my lord, but I do believe your friends are watching us."

Lord Dunbar's hands tightened their hold on her reflexively. Watching his face, Anne could not detect even a flicker of reaction. His ability to remain impassive was impressive, especially when he normally seemed to be such an open book.

~~~

Wesley felt his face freeze when he saw his friends watching them. He didn't want anyone to know they actually had a plan in place with regards to Lady Anne. It had to all look natural. He was relieved when the steps of the dance took them away from Grey and Sutton. He wished his friends were a little more capable of subtlety, but he would work with what he had.

Without a word to Anne, Wesley finished the dance with a flourish and then draped her hand through his elbow, escorting her toward his friends. It was time to follow through with his idea.

"Lady Anne, please allow me to introduce my friends. This is Lord Sebastian Grey." Grey bowed, making her an elegant leg. "And this reprobate is Lord Spencer, the fifth Earl of Sutton."

"I've already had the pleasure," the earl drawled in reply.

Anne couldn't help a little giggle at the look on the earl's face in reaction to the viscount's introduction. He raised a sardonic eyebrow, bowing his head haughtily to them both. She was just beginning to get truly nervous in his presence when she noticed the twinkle he could not quite hide shining in his eyes. With relief, she smiled widely in acknowledgement of his courteous bow.

Just as the musicians were striking up what sounded as though it were going to be a waltz, the earl bowed over Anne's hand once more. "Might I have the honour of this dance, my lady?"

Anne wasn't sure if she wanted to dance the waltz with this particular gentleman but didn't have the fortitude to refuse. Placing her hand in his, she offered up a prayer to whoever watches over misguided debutantes and followed the earl onto the dance floor.
~~~

At first, they circled the room in silence. The earl was most definitely a skilled dancer. Anne was just beginning to relax and sink into the enjoyment of the novel experience when the earl's rich baritone sounded near her ear.

"What are your intentions, my dear?"

"I beg your pardon?"

"You heard me, I'm quite certain, my lady." His cold reply sent a chill through Anne. The gentleman hadn't exactly seemed affable previously, but now she could feel the swarm of butterflies taking flight in her stomach. She made every effort to keep the panic from her face. She would hate for everyone to be able to tell that she wanted to throw up on the dance floor.

"My intentions toward what or whom, my lord?" she countered.

"Are you being intentionally daft?" he asked, annoyance evident. "Toward Dunbar. As I explained to you previously, he is my friend and like a brother to me. I will not stand by idly while some chit sinks her claws into him."

Anne's eyes grew wide as she tried to process what the earl was saying to her. "I can assure you, I am not trying to sink anything into the viscount. He has kindly offered to help me with a situation I face. I accepted his offer. He was of the opinion that you, as his friend, would be willing to help him." She broke off as fear surged into her throat. She was trying so desperately not to be a ninny, but it was terribly difficult to break a lifetime of habits in the space of a week.

"Are you trying to use guilt in order to gain my cooperation?"

Anne kept her gaze fixed on his expertly tied cravat. It was much better for her nerves than looking the earl in the face. "I am not actually trying to gain your cooperation, my lord. This whole idea can be laid at Lord Dunbar's feet. I would never have thought of such a thing on my own. He thought it would be brilliant and that you would help. It is perfectly all right if you do not wish to. I will be no further behind with or without your help, my lord."

She could feel the earl's piercing gaze searching her face, but she still could not make herself meet his eyes. Anne had no idea what he was thinking, but thankfully he did not leave her in suspense for long. "I will be keeping an eye on you, my lady, do not doubt it. But Dunbar has asked for my help, and I have promised to provide it. See that you don't make me regret it."

Anne didn't have any idea how to answer these words and heaved a sigh of relief as she heard the music slowing to an end. She pasted a smile onto her face as they strolled to the edge of the dance floor. Before she had a chance to even muster up some sort of farewell for the earl, Lord Grey was there asking for her hand for the next song.

"You are a skilled dancer, my lady," Grey complimented, making Anne's cheeks heat up.

"Thank you, my lord, it is easy to dance when you have a skilled partner."

"You must have had a lot of practice since you have been in London."

Anne was beginning to suspect the nobleman's affability was merely a ploy to get her to relax. She could feel the very opposite happening and almost stumbled as he guided her into the next turn. She stifled her sigh and decided she'd had enough of her cowardice for the evening. After taking a deep breath, she lifted her chin and looked the nobleman in the eye before stating, "His Grace, the Duke of Wrentham, and the Viscount of Bracondale are very lucky to have friends like you and the earl. And you are lucky to have them. Surely you realize that an insignificant female such as me could pose no real threat to either of them."

"I am so sorry to have to disagree with you, my lady. A female such as you poses a very definite danger." Lord Grey countered his assessment with a charming smile, but Anne was not side tracked. She held his gaze and returned his smile with a tight one of her own.

They moved around the room in silence while Grey looked innocent and unconcerned, and Anne battled with her anxiety. Finally, she mustered up the gumption to demand, "In what way could I be considered dangerous?"

"A lovely young woman with a mind of her own and a desire for marriage is a distinct threat to any gentleman wishing to hang onto his unwedded state, my lady, I am sure you realize that." Lord Grey's reasonable tone made Anne grit her teeth.

"I thought the viscount had been clear that I was not setting my cap at any of you. He had proposed that the three of you paying attention to me will draw the notice of other gentlemen who are of a mind to marry."

"But you clearly do not understand the male mind, my dear. And that is where your threat lies. There are two things about men that worry me about you. Men are competitive creatures, so one or more of us may not take well to the attentions of the other gentlemen after we have been spending time with you. As well, our dear friend Wrentham has beaten it into our heads that we must at all times act the gentleman around gently bred females such as you, and that could lead us astray in too many ways to number."

Anne blinked owlishly at her dance partner and was certain she must look like a simpleton, but she did not understand a word of what he had just said. She told him as much. "I am aware you were speaking the English language, my lord, but I fear your meaning was not at all clear to me."

"That is just as well, my dear. Pay me no mind. I have decided that it does not matter if you are a threat. Dunbar is correct, Wrentham would expect us to help you, so we shall. And we shall no doubt quite enjoy ourselves in the process." With that pronouncement, Lord Grey put an end to their discussion by increasing the vigour of their steps and swirling her around the floor with a flourish, drawing more attentive eyes toward them.

Knowing it was all part of the plan, Anne admonished herself not to allow the attention to go to her head. *Wouldn't that just seal my fall into ignominy if I were to fall for one of the trio,* she thought with horror.

Instead of escorting her back to her aunt, Lord Grey kept her hand and tucked it into his elbow. "Come along, my lady. You surely must need a drink after all this dancing." He didn't wait for her to reply as he headed to the refreshment room.

They sipped the surprisingly tasty punch and exchanged pleasantries for a moment while the crowds around them shifted and jostled. Anne felt the speculative gazes upon her and fought against the regret that she had agreed to this plan.

Lord Grey must have read her mind. "Do not turn lily livered on us now, my lady, we are just getting to the good part. Give it a couple more minutes and you shall see."

True to his words, less than five minutes later, a gentleman that Anne was sure she had been introduced to but could not for the life of her remember his name approached to request her hand for the quadrille that was about to form in the ballroom. With a curtsy to Grey, Anne left on the other gentleman's arm.

Anne spent the rest of the night on the dance floor. It was the first time in her life that she did not spend a single minute as a wallflower. It sent a satisfied thrill to the very centre of her feminine soul, despite the fact it had been orchestrated by the viscount. Even other ladies were appearing to be friendlier towards her, no doubt in an effort to snag some of the gentlemen for themselves, but Anne didn't care what the reasons were, she was enjoying nearly every moment of the evening.

The only fly in the ointment was the anxious feeling she got whenever she felt the viscount's watchful gaze following her. She doubted he meant to do so, but she felt as though he were waiting to see if she would fail. She decided to call him out on his behaviour. Instead of ignoring his eyes upon her, she met his gaze and offered him as dazzling a smile as she could muster. She wanted to grin when he blinked and turned away.

Her grin died a quick death, however, when the gentleman she was dancing with led her to the side of the dance floor and she discovered the viscount was there waiting for her.

"I do believe this is to be our turn, my lady," he said as he bowed over her hand.

Anne didn't have the nerve to contradict his words, so there was nothing she could do except put her hand in his and follow him back onto the dance floor. She couldn't gage his mood, so she kept silent as they were swept into the rhythm of the music. They circled the room once, twice, before he finally broke the silence.

"You seem to be enjoying yourself," he offered conversationally.

"I am," she agreed without going into detail. She kept a pleasant smile on her face and avoided his eyes.

"And our plan seems to be working out rather well," he continued, as though she had said nothing.

"That's true," she acknowledged as well, a small smile finally dawning on her lips.

She allowed her eyes to rise to meet his, and it was as though he had been waiting for that moment. His gaze ensnared hers and held it. It felt to her as though he could read her soul while he stared into her eyes.

"What is going on inside that head of yours?" he asked softly.

She tried to blank her thoughts so he couldn't read her mind, but she couldn't hide it. Instead of excluding him, she tried to seem unconcerned. She lifted her shoulder in a small shrug despite the steps of the dance. She finally admitted to him what was making her uncomfortable.

"I'm not enjoying you watching my every step as though you think I'm a villain, my lord. While it is true that I agreed to try to entrap the duke into marriage, I had no intention of hurting him. Now that I have been made aware of the fact that I had been thoughtless to the point of foolishness, I am making every effort to be a more thoughtful person. You do not need to fear for the gentlemen of the *ton*."

"I have no idea what you're talking about, my lady. I realize when I first confronted you that is exactly what I thought, but now that I have gotten to know you better I am quite convinced that you won't be hurting anyone."

"Then why do you keep watching me at every opportunity?" Anne was frustrated with his lack of sense.

"Because I fear that someone else is going to hurt *you*."

Anne could only blink at him in silence. It had never occurred to her that he could have such a concern. She actually giggled at the thought.

"It is hardly a matter for laughter, my lady," he objected.

This only made her giggle harder. "I apologize, my lord, but you really are not making much sense. But never mind. Our dance is about to end. You needn't worry about me. I have my aunt and uncle to look after me, my lord. Have no fear."

Chapter Five

Lord Manfred Austen had never felt so vile in all his life. He was lying in a puddle on the side of the road somewhere. He wasn't even completely sure where he was. The ruffians who had beaten him and left him had driven him some distance out of Town, he was fairly sure. They no doubt thought he was dead. He almost wished that he were. It probably wouldn't hurt to breathe if he were dead.

He shook his head ever so slightly to rid himself of the useless thought. He needed to pull himself together. Before those cretins had jumped him, he had been promising himself to get some gumption and be the man his daughter needed him to be. He needed to reject the negative thoughts and attempt to survive long enough to tell her how proud he was of her and hopefully see her set up in a better life than he had been able to provide for her up until now.

The sound of a horse plodding along the road approached. Austen wondered if he should be hopeful or fearful. He decided to stay still and wait to see what happened. He held his breath.

That might not have been the best idea as he may have lost consciousness. The next thing he was aware of there was a soft feminine voice calling to him. He couldn't make much sense of the words as he felt himself being hoisted up and placed almost gently somewhere. He knew nothing else.

Sometime later, he awoke as strong hands were turning him onto a soft bed. He heard the soft voice uttering commands. Austen told himself he ought to speak, whether to protest or express appreciation, but he was still too weak.

The next thing he knew, bright sunshine was streaming into the room and he felt decidedly better. With effort, Austen cracked his eyes open to survey his environment.

"Oh, my dear man, praise be, you've returned to the land of the living. Lawks, the Miss will have my head for waking you, but I say it's time and enough that you need to be waking up. It's not right for a body to sleep that long. Especially if you was hit in the head. Were you hit in the head, sir?"

"I do believe I was, yes." Austen winced over the scratchy sound of his voice.

"Oh, lawks, sir, let me get you something to drink."

Austen peered at the portly woman as she lifted his shoulders comfortably and helped him tilt the cup to drizzle some broth down his throat. The liquid felt heavenly as it eased along his parched lips and throat. He couldn't help sighing with relief.

"Now, I'd best be getting the Miss. She'll want to see to you for herself. You just stay put, mister, and I'll be right back."

Before he could object, she bustled from the room.

Within moments, she returned with the most beautiful woman he had ever seen. He thought he was perhaps still unconscious, she was that pretty. But then he remembered he was not an imaginative man. His mind would not have been able to conjure so much beauty on its own. Austen would have grinned at her like a simpleton if it would not hurt so much.

The angelic vision approached the bed, staring at him intently for a moment. She smiled at him, and he thought for a moment he was going to lose consciousness again. He wondered then how hard he had been hit by those clods. He was not at all the type to wax poetic about a woman, no matter how lovely her appearance. He shifted his eyes away to avoid the glare of her attraction.

And then she opened her mouth. It felt to Austen as though warm honey flowed over him as she spoke, and he knew he had lost his mind when he was beaten.

"You don't look so well, mister. You really shouldn't be sitting up," the vision was saying to him as he closed his eyes and nodded. "Is there anyone we should contact for you? Will your family be worried when you didn't come home last night?"

Austen kept his eyes closed and felt misery swamp him as he thought of his dear Anne. She probably was wondering where he was, but hopefully she was having such a good time with her aunt that she wasn't paying him much mind. Her aunt and uncle certainly wouldn't be too worried about him, since it was their suggestion that made him leave in the first place.

He realized he hadn't answered the woman's question and opened his eyes for a moment only to shut them again when they encountered her warm grey gaze. "No, I don't think anyone will be overly anxious about my absence." He paused for a moment before realizing he was no doubt being a burden. "Although, I really ought to be removing myself, as I have no wish to overstay my welcome."

"Not at all, mister. It's no bother at all. But you really ought to tell us your name. It's a little awkward for us to keep calling you mister." Her low chuckle actually sent a tremble through his belly. He was acting like a debutante!

He needed to stop this imbecilic behaviour and get a grip back on his life, not only for his daughter but also for himself. This mess with Broderick had shown him that he had truly hit bottom. The look on his daughter's face when she had fully realized what he had tried to get her to do was something he never wanted to see again for the rest of his days. He opened his eyes and did his best to ignore the feelings the woman before him generated.

"My name is Lord Manfred Austen, Viscount of Rowanwood." He saw her eyes widen, and he was able to utter a self-deprecating laugh. "That sounds so much more important than it is. Rowanwood is falling down around our ears, and I am currently waiting while my only daughter enjoys her first Season and hopefully manages to catch the eye of a wealthy gentleman willing to settle funds on her family." He felt the heat of embarrassment climbing his cheeks at what he had admitted to this stranger.

Her low chuckle sounded again. "I do believe you are still feeling the effects of your beating, my lord. My name is Mrs. Kate Appleton, and you are welcome to stay here as long as you need to recover. My housekeeper, Mrs. Peabody, has been looking after you since you got here last night and assures me that she would be delighted to continue to do so. We shall leave you now to let you rest a little more and will return to check on you in an hour or so."

Austen didn't think he would be able to sleep any more, but within minutes of the two women leaving the room he was fast asleep. It felt like only moments later, but from the quality of the light he could see through the window, it was now mid or late afternoon so he knew hours had passed. He felt remarkably better and thought about getting out of the bed. His thoughts must have conjured his caretakers because in that moment the door opened and Mrs. Peabody stepped into the room with Mrs. Appleton right behind her.

"Lawks, my lord, you sure look a sight better than you did when you were last awake. It seems to me that you're going to survive the ordeal. Would you care for a meal now that you're a wee bit better?"

Before he could even answer her, his stomach let out a loud growl that made the heat climb again into his cheeks but made them all chuckle as well. "That would be most appreciated, Mrs. Peabody, thank you," he answered formally, ignoring his discomfort. He might have downgraded himself to a scoundrel, but he was still a gentleman at heart.

"Missy here will keep you company while I hurry down to the kitchen to fetch you something."

Mrs. Appleton looked as though she wanted to protest, but then she smiled warmly and took a seat on the chair placed at the end of the bed. Austen smiled as he noted the housekeeper had left the door wide open in an attempt to lend respectability to the fact that Mrs. Appleton was in a man's bedchamber. Of course, her being a Mrs. made it much less of an issue. He wondered absently where Mr. Appleton was.

"Do you remember what happened to you, Lord Austen? Would you like me to have the local magistrate call by so you can have an investigation launched?"

Austen shrugged. "I remember what happened, but I doubt the magistrate will have much to say about it. I got drunk and a couple of ruffians decided to relieve me of my purse. When they discovered that it was empty, they took their frustrations out on my person. While I might be able to provide a description, I doubt it would be specific enough not to be any one of a hundred labourers from anywhere around these parts."

The beautiful woman nodded sagely. "You are probably right, more's the pity. Well, I am sorry you have had to bear the brunt of their stupidity, but perhaps you have seen the error of your ways and can now return to your life and not look for solutions at the bottom of an ale glass."

Her tone had not been censorious, so Austen took no offense. Besides, he had just been thinking the same thing. He had to laugh despite the fact that it hurt his face to do so. "You may be right, Mrs. Appleton. I do believe they have beaten some sense into me."

Her rich warm chuckle joined his even as she blushed. "I did not mean to imply that you lacked for sense, my lord."

"Perhaps you didn't, but you should have because I surely did. I mean to change all that as soon as I can. But first, I do believe I shall have to take advantage of your hospitality for just a little longer or I don't think I could make it back to Town."

"We are happy to have you as long as you need," she assured him.

"Are you certain Mr. Appleton won't mind?" He hoped he sounded nonchalant as he asked.

Mrs. Appleton looked flustered as she answered. "There is no longer a Mr. Appleton, I'm afraid. But I'm fairly certain he would not have begrudged a helping hand to someone in need."

Mrs. Peabody chose that moment to bustle back into the room bearing a tray with a steaming bowl of hearty-looking soup and a thick slice of bread with butter. "This should put some colour back into your skin, my lord, but shouldn't be too hard for your innards to handle after the trouble they've been through. Now, eat up," she scolded him as though he were a schoolboy, much to Austen's delight. He hadn't had anyone to care for him since his wife died except his daughter, and she was not the hearty type.

The housekeeper bustled around the room while Austen ate, twitching his quilts straight and plumping his pillows. Mrs. Appleton watched with raised eyebrows until her laughter brought the housekeeper to a standstill. "Whatever are you doing, Mrs. Peabody?"

The housekeeper blushed fiery red but answered honestly. "I'm fidgeting, Missy, and well you know it. It's not every day we get a gentleman to care for. I like it."

The trio all laughed over her words while Austen felt his curiosity stir. Before he had a chance to voice any of his questions, the two women exchanged a speaking glance and Mrs. Appleton got to her feet.

"We ought to let you rest some more, my lord," she said as the housekeeper gathered the tray from off his lap.

"Thank you both so much for your generous hospitality. I fear I would have shortly been dead if you had not come along and picked me up off the side of the road."

"Oh, no, my lord, I am certain someone else would have been along soon after us and would have been just as happy to help you. Everyone in these parts is a very kind, generous soul."

Austen was doubtful if anyone else would have gone to such an effort as she obviously had on his behalf, taking him into her home and nursing him back to health. He could have even wound up in jail if one of the villagers had contacted the magistrate instead of helping him to recover.

He couldn't very well tell her that though, so he just offered a neutral smile and watched them silently as they left the room.

Even though he had already been sleeping almost nonstop for more than a day, within minutes of the women leaving him, he was fast asleep and did not awake again until the early morning light was filtering into his room.

He was just blinking himself awake when there was a slight movement at the door and Mrs. Peabody stuck her head into the room. When she saw that his eyes were open, her face lit up and she came in fully.

"Good morning, my lord, how have you fared over night?"

"It would seem that I survived," he commented drily, which seemed to amuse her as a wide smile broke out onto her homely face.

"And glad we are of that," she declared with feeling. "Would you like me to bring you something to break your fast? How does your stomach feel today?"

"It actually feels quite normal and hungry," he answered, embarrassed to be discussing his body with the housekeeper.

"Very well, my lord, I shall return momentarily." She hurried away and was good as her word, back within a few short minutes.

Austen tried not to turn up his nose, but gruel was not what he had been hoping for that morning. His feelings must have been written on his face because Mrs. Peabody chuckled again but didn't change her mind.

"You need fortification, my lord, and your person has been through an ordeal. This is just what the doctor would order if you had agreed to see him."

Austen sighed but obediently picked up the spoon and ate every bite. Despite its appearance, the porridge was remarkably tasty and the warm mixture disappeared quickly, satisfying his hunger and making him feel fortified, just as she had promised it would. He was getting heartily sick of sitting in the bed and was just about to swing his feet over the side and attempt to get up when Mrs. Appleton entered the room.

"Good morning, my lord," she called to him in her melodious voice, causing him to feel a tightness in his chest. He actually reached up and rubbed it absently as he watched her walking toward him. "How are you feeling today? Do you think you might be able to get up and spare a little company?"

He brightened at her words. "I was just thinking that I couldn't bear much longer in bed." He smiled so as to not cause offense with his words.

"Excellent. Mrs. Peabody had your clothes laundered and repaired yesterday, so you should be set if you want to dress. Do you think you might need a hand?" She had puttered around the room laying out the clothes he hadn't noticed and pouring a basin of warm water so he could clean up.

"I feel much stronger today. I should be able to manage for myself, thank you." He turned to the housekeeper. "Thank you, Mrs. Peabody, for mending and washing my clothes. I shudder at the burden I have been to you fine folks."

"Lawks, get on with you, my lord," Mrs. Peabody responded with characteristic flare. "We have been enjoying the excitement. Now, if you think you'll be all right on your own, I'll just hover outside your door and you can yell for help if you need me."

Austen could feel heat climbing into his cheeks over this offer, but he didn't want to appear churlish by dismissing her. He just nodded and waited for them to file out before swinging his legs over the side of the bed.

He was ridiculously weak. No doubt the days of drinking before his beating hadn't helped his health any. Gritting his teeth, he refused to call for help. Feeling grateful that Mrs. Appleton had placed his clothing on the end of the bed, he sat on the edge and managed to get himself clothed without too much difficulty. Taking a deep, fortifying breath, he stood slowly, wavering on his feet for a moment before shuffling his way to the table with the basin of water quickly cooling.

His reflection was not reassuring, and he was glad his daughter didn't have to see him like this. His little Anne would probably have a fit of vapours if she saw him now, he thought with a fond smile that threatened to split the crack that was struggling to heal in his lip.

Once he had rinsed the sleep out of his eyes and combed his wayward hair, he was feeling much more human but was already beginning to tire. Getting below stairs was beginning to feel like it would be a test of his will, but he was determined to win the battle. He had been acting an imbecile long enough, and he was determined to turn over a new leaf.

He had decided the day before to allow the beating to have beaten some sense into him. He needed to start showing that sense by not becoming a leech on his new friends. He had no intention of repaying their kindness by taking advantage of it. He needed to regain his strength and get on with his life. Getting back to his daughter to ensure she was not being led astray by her aunt and uncle had to be a priority for him.

He gritted his teeth once more, let go of the table's edge, and shuffled his way to the bedchamber door.

"Lawks almighty, my lord, I was starting to wonder if I'd have to come in and fetch you. But here you are looking almost none the worse for the wear. Very good. Shall I give you my arm as we make our way down the stairs or do you think you can manage them on your own?"

Austen wasn't sure what was written on his face at her words, but his rejection of her suggestion must have been evident because the housekeeper laughed and launched into speech again. "I do apologize, my lord, it's just that exciting to have someone to hover over. You must excuse me. Never mind my fidgets, you can just hold onto the railing if you think you might need some support. But I'll just be here beside you."

"Thank you, Mrs. Peabody," he replied as graciously as he could muster. He tried not to wince as he took each step slowly, but the effort was costing him. He could feel a trickle of sweat making its way down his back as he steadily progressed down the seemingly interminable staircase.

When he finally reached the bottom, he paused to catch his breath but then had the prickly sensation of being watched. Turning his head abruptly, he was surprised to see Mrs. Appleton standing in the doorway of what appeared to be a sitting room. It looked as though she were waiting for him.

"Are you quite all right, my lord?" she asked solicitously. "I do hope it was worth the effort. Would you care for any sort of refreshment? A cold drink or a cup of tea?"

"A cup of coffee would actually be just the thing if it would not be too much trouble," he answered with a hopeful glance as he made an effort to step smartly, rather than the shuffle he had been doing in the bedroom. Even disgraced noblemen who have hit rock bottom have their pride to keep up in front of beautiful women.

Mrs. Peabody bustled past him. "I shall see to it right away, Missy."

Austen finally found a reason to laugh despite his pains. "Why does your housekeeper call you Missy? Was I mistaken when I heard you introduce yourself as Mrs. Appleton?" He placed gentle emphasis on the Mrs. when he spoke.

"No, you were not mistaken," she replied with a little sigh. "It is just that servants who have known you since your birth have a difficult time acknowledging that you are no longer a child."

"Ah, yes, I have a similar situation with the butler at home," Austen acknowledged. "So even though you married, you are still in the home you grew up in?" he asked, trying not to let on the depths of his curiosity about the woman.

"That is correct, my lord. I was an only child, and my husband was a soldier. We never really had much of a marriage or life on our own. When my parents passed away, I just kept on living here."

"I'm sorry for your losses, madam. You seem to be a remarkably positive individual despite your many sorrows."

"Doing anything else doesn't make it any better, does it?"

"No," he replied, "And I can answer that from experience."

"What do you mean?"

He didn't know what it was about her, but before he could put a bridle on his lips he was telling her his life story. He tried to make the long story as short as possible but wasn't sure he succeeded. "I was already running adrift, but when my wife died I just seemed to lose all control of myself. I began drinking more heavily and made some poor financial choices under the guise of trying to right matters. Now I have placed my daughter in a precarious position. Thankfully she has her maternal aunt, who is sponsoring her for the Season and is keeping an eye on her while I fall apart. But I feel wretched about letting her down. When my daughter's uncle suggested that it might be better if I make myself scarce, I agreed with him and went on this most recent bender."

He paused for a moment, looking out the window in an effort to avoid her sympathetic gaze as he divulged his disgrace. "But now I can see how badly I have let my poor daughter down, and I feel determined to return to Town and make it up to her. I wish I could also assure her that we don't need the money and for her to remain unwed until such a time as she is of a mind to marry, but I'm not sure if that would be completely true. I have made such a muck of things that I'm not sure if I can manage for the both of us."

He finally stopped talking. He had heard that confession was good for the soul, but he was merely feeling wrung out from baring himself to this woman. Her sympathetic silence was a little comforting, but he still couldn't meet her eyes for his shame.

"Well, it seems to me that nothing yet is irreversible. Perhaps you ought to discuss it with your daughter and see what her thoughts are on the matter."

Austen smiled. "Until recently I would have told you I don't expect her to have many thoughts on the matter, but her reaction to the scam I tried to involve her in makes me think she has more going on in her mind than she lets on."

"Most women do," Mrs. Appleton replied with a gentle smile. "Ah, Mrs. Peabody, your timing is impeccable. I think now is the perfect time for a cup of your delicious coffee."

The aging viscount was happy to allow the heavy moment to pass and drank appreciatively of the strong brew. It was just what he needed to help shake the cobwebs from his abused mind. After a few minutes of companionable silence, his hostess looked between him and the window.

"It's a beautiful day outside. How are you feeling? Are you up for taking the air and seeing a little bit of my farm?"

"I would love to go outside, madam, but I am afraid I will be moving at a snail's pace."

"That's quite all right. I have already seen to most of my chores for the day, so I do not have anything urgent calling for my attention."

Austen again felt a strange flutter in his chest when he spied her warm smile directed at him. It had been so long since he had felt attracted to a woman that for a moment he thought his health was having a setback. When his mind slowly realized what the sensation truly was, he felt fiery heat climb into his cheeks. He was glad she was busying herself with the coffee things and didn't notice his discomfort.

He had no desire to repay her kindness by burdening her with unwelcome advances. He decided it would be best if he could take his leave of this place as soon as possible. Unfortunately, since he had no funds, he was unsure how he would manage to leave. If he were completely healthy, he could just walk back to Town, even if it took him several days. But in his current state, he would probably keel over before he made it to the next village. He gritted his teeth and determined to be as little a burden as possible.

He was still mulling over the problem as Mrs. Appleton led him out into the bright fall day.

"See how beautiful it is?" she enthused.

"I can see that," he replied as he gazed at her. He realized his tone must have been a little too warm as her eyes flew to meet his and then her gaze faltered. He cursed himself as every manner of fool before he quickly changed the subject by asking her about the property.

"This farm has been in my family for a little over a century. My great-great-grandfather performed some sort of service for the king and was granted this land. It came with no title, but it has served our family well."

"I can imagine," Austen agreed. "What did your ancestor do for the king?"

Mrs. Appleton shrugged. "No one knows. There has been wild speculation through the years but apparently, my great-great-grandfather refused to tell anyone, not even his wife. It would seem secrecy was part of the deal."

"What a delicious mystery." Austen smiled. "Did you have no siblings?"

"Sadly no. My mother died when I was young, and my father chose not to remarry. His nephew, my cousin, is starting to eye my property, expecting that it will pass to him or his son one day since my husband died before we were able to have any children."

"You are still young. Surely you can remarry."

"I could, but I would really rather someone wished to marry me for my sake rather than to get their hands on my property."

Austen laughed. "You have the opposite problem from my daughter. Perhaps you should come to London with me and have a conversation with Anne. I do believe it would be most enlightening."

Mrs. Appleton's gaze again flickered to meet his. He couldn't quite read what was going through her mind, but the butterflies began their incessant fluttering once more.

"I have never been to London, my lord. I would have no idea how to go on. But I'm sure your daughter is lovely and shall do just fine without any words of wisdom I might be able to impart." She then changed the subject by leading him to the barns.

"I have cut back somewhat on the scope of our farming as my needs are simple and I found it a bit much to keep up with. Do you farm on your property, my lord?"

"Just enough to keep food on the table. I'm afraid I have let everything run to rack and ruin. I would be grateful if you could give me some advice, actually. I really do need to pull myself up by my bootstraps if it is not already too late."

"I don't believe it's ever too late if you're willing to put in a bit of effort."

"I think I'm willing, but I will need to gain a little bit more strength before I can put in any effort."

"My men would be happy to show you whatever you might want to know."

Austen felt hope stirring again in his chest as he smiled gratefully at his hostess. It was beginning to appear as though his attack were the best thing that could have happened to him.

Chapter Six

Meanwhile, back in London

"Lord Dunbar to see you, my lady," the butler announced solemnly as he ushered the viscount into the already crowded receiving room.

Anne glanced up at him from the settee she was seated upon and quickly got to her feet. She dipped into a brief curtsy as he approached to take her hand. She watched his gaze circling the room but she was unable interpret the look on his face. It was a strange combination of delight and irritation.

"It is lovely to see you this morning, my lady," he greeted her as he bowed formally over her hand.

She pulled her hand quickly out of his, annoyed by the thrill that went through her at his touch. Certainly she should be getting used to it by now. She scolded herself while she tried to keep a neutral expression on her face.

"And you, my lord. I'm sure you are familiar with everyone present. The housekeeper has just brought us tea. Could I pour you a cup?"

"No, thank you. I have just left the breakfast table, myself. I had actually called round to see if you would care to accompany me for a drive. I did not expect to find you quite so occupied."

The curl of his lip indicated he was not quite pleased to find her so, but Anne reasoned this was the purpose of their plan, so it was ridiculous for her to feel guilty. She offered him a bland smile.

"I would have loved to accompany you, my lord, but as you can see…" She allowed her words to trail off, unsure of the proper etiquette for such a situation, as she had never found herself in need of juggling multiple visitors. She was relieved from further comment by the butler announcing yet another arrival.

"Lord Sebastian Grey, my lady," the butler declared while someone across the room hailed the viscount. He stepped away, allowing Anne to greet the latest arrival.

"My lord," she greeted Sebastian simply with a shallow curtsy.

"Lady Anne," he hailed heartily. "You are looking radiant today. None the worse for your late night of dancing, I am happy to note."

Anne felt a blush stealing over her features but kept her smile firmly in place. She continued to struggle with the desire to hide behind the nearest curtain. She'd had no idea how gruelling it was to be the centre of attention. Taking a deep breath, she turned to the young lady at her side and introduced her to Sebastian. That young lady expertly launched into a practiced flirtation with the aristocratic gentleman, allowing Anne to slip away.

She could feel the viscount's gaze burning into her shoulder blades, but she refused to glance in his direction as she made every effort to enjoy a conversation with another debutante about the ball they had attended the night before.

"Wasn't the music just divine?" Charlotte trilled. "And the punch! It was not nearly as tepid as usual. I do believe the Clairhurst ball was one of the best I have yet attended."

"I would have to agree with you," Anne replied. For her, it was the first time she had ever enjoyed a ball, so it wouldn't have mattered what the music or punch was like. In fact, she could not recall anything about the musicians except that there had been no glaring errors in any of the pieces they had played.

"Are you not having the time of your life, Lady Anne?" the young woman continued to enthuse.

"It is certainly a delight," Anne answered and then returned, "What about you, Miss Charlotte?"

"Oh, my lady, it is everything I knew it would be," Charlotte gushed before launching into her tales of wonder for the Season.

Anne could feel mirth rising in her chest and wondered how she was going to prevent herself from laughing out loud at the other young woman. Blessedly, before she lost her composure completely, some of her guests began to take their leave. As nearly everyone in Society followed the lead of others, it didn't take too long before the room was nearly empty.

Lord Grey was second to last to bow over her hand. His eyes were dancing as he kissed her wrist with a flourish. "You are a decidedly popular young woman, my lady. It is an honour to know you."

She couldn't help but to giggle over his words. "You are a jester, my lord."

"Not at all," he declared before he took his leave after exchanging a quizzical glance with Lord Dunbar, the only other remaining occupant of the room.

Sebastian left the door open as he let himself out of the room. Anne turned to the viscount, expecting him to also take his leave. His words surprised her.

"You mentioned that you would be happy to accompany me on a drive. Now that all your admirers have made themselves scarce, would you do me the honour?"

Anne felt a thrill travel up her spine at his words but tried to hang onto reason. "I would hate to keep you from anything important, my lord. You have already done enough to launch me successfully into Society. Do you think it is really necessary?"

It appeared as though her words irritated the viscount. "Necessary or not, I extended you an invitation, my lady. Do not be missish about it."

Feeling her flush spread to the roots of her hair, Anne stammered out a hasty acceptance. "I will just let my aunt know that I will be leaving and change into something more appropriate for a drive, my lord. If you would wait a few minutes, I shall endeavour to be as quick as possible."

"Very well, I shall await you here."

Anne hurried from the room. She found her aunt in the room she liked to refer to as her boudoir grinning like Miss Charlotte. "Oh my dear, you are a success. I don't know how you did it, but I'm sure it is because your father hasn't been around glaring at any potential suitors. Isn't it marvellous?"

She had to blink before she could respond appropriately to her aunt's words. After a moment's hesitation, she chose to ignore them all, merely informing her of the viscount's invitation.

"Well, do not leave the gentleman waiting, you silly girl, get on with it. Oh, this is so exciting."

Anne left her aunt as quickly as she had arrived, unable to bear watching her clapping her hands with delight over her supposed conquest of the viscount. She didn't know how she would be able to break the news to her that the viscount wasn't about to offer for her.

Her maid had been informed in that inexplicable way that servants always knew everything that was going on and was waiting for Anne when she got to her room. She already had a riding habit ready for her to change into.

"Thank you, Sally," Anne said, not bothering to question how she knew what was needed. Within minutes she was changed and her hair had been combed and extra pins were inserted to ensure it held up to the rigours of wind.

"I am impressed, my lady," Wesley complimented as Anne re-joined him in the receiving room. "Most young ladies would have taken at least twice as long."

"Would you like me to leave and return in a few minutes?" she asked, allowing her sarcasm to show.

Wesley grinned. "Not at all, my lady. My horses will be glad not to be left waiting any longer than necessary." With those words, he led the way to the door.

Within moments, they were making their way rapidly through the centre of the city. Anne was surprised to see they were not heading in the direction of Hyde Park.

"Where are we going, my lord?" she asked, hesitant to break the silence that had descended but curious about their destination.

"I thought a drive out into the country would make you comfortable. I do hope that meets with your approval."

Anne was surprised by the viscount's slightly abrasive behaviour. She began to feel wary about spending time with him. She really knew very little about the nobleman and wondered if it had been wise to accept his invitation to essentially be alone with him. The viscount's servant hanging onto the back of the carriage would be of little assistance to her should she require it. She hoped to keep her disquiet to herself and merely nodded her acceptance of his words.

Several moments passed before the viscount spoke up, sounding impatient. "Are you giving me the silent treatment, my lady?"

Anne nearly wrenched her neck as she swung her gaze rapidly around to look at him. "Not at all, my lord," she protested. She paused in discomfort before admitting, "I am uncertain of your mood, my lord, and have no idea what to say to you. You have to realize I am deeply grateful for your assistance and have no intention of returning your kindness with mistreatment."

The viscount's fierce demeanour instantly changed at her words. "Oh, Lady Anne, you need not apologize. It is me that owes you an explanation. I am the one being churlish. It was just so unexpected to see your rooms overflowing with posturing dandies and silly debutantes. It was foolish of me to blame you for that. It was obvious, at least to me, that you were as surprised by the hordes as I was."

"But surely you expected me to have callers, my lord. Was it not your intention to bring attention to me?" Anne was confused by the viscount's admission.

She was surprised to see spots of colour appear on the viscount's cheekbones in response to her observation. "I will admit freely that I had not fully thought the matter through. You are quite correct, though. I should have expected your popularity to result in callers. But never mind about my mawkish behaviour. Tell me, how did it feel to be inundated with callers?"

Anne thought for a moment, trying to decide for herself how she felt about it. "I am very much of two minds on the subject, my lord. I did not expect your plan to have such marked results, especially not this quickly. I knew you and Lords Grey and Spencer had influence amongst the *ton*, but I had no idea you could so quickly transform me from wallflower to popular in one evening. I think I would appreciate it a little more if it had taken more effort. This just demonstrates what followers everyone is."

"You are quite right, my dear, but please do not consider it to be an insult or any reflection upon you."

"I don't. It is clearly not a reflection upon me in either direction. I realize my current popularity and my prior lack of it had very little to do with me as an individual. But it does make me wonder if any one of those gentlemen will actually follow through and offer for me. If they are merely following the crowd, it seems rather doubtful. Not one of them seemed genuinely interested in learning anything about me."

"Give it time, my lady," the viscount soothed. "Let us just enjoy our drive and put our cares behind us for the time being."

Anne eyed him askance. "Are you truly certain this is not taking you from other, more important matters, my lord? I know you are a busy gentleman and not the idle fellow you allow others to think you."

"And how do you know that?" he demanded as he turned his gaze toward her.

She tried not to quail under that searching gaze of his. Shrugging, she answered him truthfully. "Being a wallflower allowed me to observe those around me. I learned to read the signs."

"What signs?" Now the viscount appeared fascinated by her words.

"For example, while your cravat is tied precisely and just as fancifully as the other gentlemen who visited this morning, you did not once stare into the mirror and twitch it unlike each and every one of them. And I couldn't help but notice that you spent far more time listening than blathering on about nonsense, again unlike the other gentlemen present. And I did overhear Lord Grey asking you about something in the House. I assumed this was the House of Lords he was mentioning."

The viscount had his eyebrow raised in a sardonic gesture before he relaxed and chuckled when she paused in her faltering list. "I am impressed, my lady. You are not the idle debutante that everyone is expecting either. Nor the country mouse you think yourself to be. I think the Home Office would do well to secure you for your powers of observation."

Anne felt the heat rising once more in her cheeks. She shook her head in denial. "I have been on my own for so long that I am finding observing so many people to be absolutely fascinating," she excused.

"Do not make light, my dear. Most of the young ladies have been in very similar circumstances as you, and they have taken to gossip readily, not observing intelligently as you seem to be doing."

Heaving a sigh, Anne asked rather plaintively, "Do you think a gentleman will offer for me who might appreciate that I am trying to improve as a person?"

"Whatever do you mean?"

Shrugging, Anne wasn't sure how to explain her thoughts. "I do observe things, but I haven't been much in the habit of thinking about what I observed. The result is that I almost went through with a plot to entrap a duke into marrying me. Now that I have had a chance to think on it, I realize that it would have been a disaster. Can you imagine?" She shuddered delicately as she thought about it. "You know the duke. How would he have felt if he had ended up married to me and then found out afterward that it had all been a plot arranged by my father and one of his so-called friends?"

"He would have been furious."

"See what I mean?"

"But he would never have mistreated you for it, no matter how angry he was."

"You are a loyal friend to the duke, my lord, but even if he did not mistreat me, I cannot imagine he would have been happy with me, and it certainly would not have made a good foundation for our marriage." She paused for a moment of reflection and then carried on, her tone pensive.

"I want to learn to think deeply about things, my lord. But I fear that many gentlemen prefer if women don't think. You saw all those callers in my aunt's receiving room. Very few of them were thinking about anything besides the cut of their coat, the strong lines of the latest race horses, or which events they are to attend this evening. I am not certain this plan of ours is going to attract the sort of gentleman who will make me a good mate."

She paused again but then realized she was probably sounding ungrateful. "I do not mean to sound as though I don't appreciate what you have done!"

Turning to him earnestly, she placed her hand on his arm as he held the reins. She wished she could pull her hand back, as she felt a jolt where her hand rested. It almost distracted her from her line of thought, but she pulled herself together and continued.

"Really, in my current circumstances, I should just be grateful if I will have a choice of gentlemen rather than just whichever one might be willing to take me."

~~~

Wesley could not take her melancholy manner any longer. He transferred both reins into one hand and placed his other hand over hers where it rested on his arm. He wanted only to comfort her and had to fight the inappropriate urge to take her into his arms. He satisfied himself with patting her hand as he said, "Do not work yourself up into a taking, my lady. We shall find you the perfect spouse." He could not find in himself any enthusiasm for the search, though, so he decided to change the subject. "There was an unrelated matter that I wanted to discuss with you, which is partially why I asked you on this drive. I arranged for a Runner to search for your father."

This must have been exactly the right thing to say as she brightened considerably at his words and turned her shining grey gaze to meet his. "And have you heard anything yet, my lord?"

"As a matter of fact, that is why I have chosen this particular route. I have reason to believe your father might have spent a day or two in the village we are about to enter."

Anne bounced a little in the seat beside him. "Oh, how delightful! Do you think he might still be here?"

"Not from what I've heard, but I wanted you to be able to confirm with me if we are on the right track."

Wesley was surprised when she looked up at him with a grin, but there were tears clearly glistening in her eyes. Alarmed, he demanded, "Whatever is wrong?"

"Nothing at all, my lord. I am so happy that my cheeks hurt. No one has ever done anything so kind for me before."

This made Wesley decidedly uncomfortable. It had taken almost no effort on his part to have his secretary arrange for a Runner. But her obvious appreciation made him feel as though his chest were swelling. It was an unfamiliar sensation, but he
~~~

quite liked it. He felt like grinning but managed to contain himself.

"That is a rather sad state of affairs, my dear, as I have hardly done anything yet. I hope I haven't gotten your hopes raised unduly. You do realize that we are unlikely to find your father today, do you not?"

She nodded her confirmation, but then a tear tumbled down her cheeks and she offered a watery chuckle. "Have no fear, my lord, I promise I shan't treat you to a fit of the vapours. And yes, I do realize that we will not find him today. I am just so excited that we are on the way to finding him, and this feels like I am finally having an adventure." She turned to him with widened eyes. "I actually think that is why I fell for my father's scheme. I wanted an adventure. This is a much better idea for an acceptable adventure. Thank you, my lord."

Wesley joined her in her delightful laughter. They rode along in companionable silence for a couple more minutes before she turned to him with her cute little nose wrinkled in puzzlement.

"Have you any idea where we are, my lord? I confess that I was not properly paying attention when we left Town and have lost track of which direction we are headed in." She paused and released another tinkle of laughter before continuing. "I know a proper outdoors woman would be able to say much more than just that from the angle of the sun we are heading west, but that is about all I can tell."

Wesley couldn't help but burst into laughter. He could tell his amusement embarrassed her, for which he felt badly, but it was difficult to quell his amusement. When he could finally contain his mirth, he complimented her. "Very good, my lady! We *are* heading west. And we are about to enter the town of Uxbridge. A lovely village, Uxbridge is. Have you ever been there?"

He was surprised that his question brought bright colour to her cheeks. Thankfully, she did not leave him in doubt about her thoughts.

"My lord, surely you realize I have barely been anywhere. If it was not on the way from our estate to London when my father brought me for the Season then I have not been there."

Wesley clucked in sympathy. "Well, then you are in for a treat. I am certain you shall enjoy Uxbridge."

"Truly, my lord? Why do you say so?"

He found her to be a delightful companion. She seemed so easy to please that afternoon. "It is quaint and inviting and there are several shops I would expect a lady such as yourself would enjoy frequenting. And I know from first-hand experience that there is an inn at the centre of town whose cook makes pastries to rival anything you could find at Gunther's fine establishment. So, once we have spoken to the innkeeper where your father spent some time, I will treat you to some tea before we head back to Town."

Wesley was surprised to receive her silent stare at the conclusion of his statement. "Does that not meet with your approval, my lady?" he prompted her.

"Of course, it does, my lord. I am just left to wonder why you are being so kind to me. It was just days ago that you considered me to be an enemy. Now you are going out of your way to be my friend. It is disconcerting, I must say."

Again, Wesley laughed. "You have just answered your own question. As odd as it might seem, you have become my friend. I find that I quite like you despite the fact that we got off to a rocky start."

Anne again wrinkled her nose at him. "Can destitute debutantes whose fathers display highly questionable judgment be friends with highly sought after bachelor viscounts?"

"Absolutely," Wesley declared emphatically. "Why not?"

Wesley heard her sigh before she answered. "By rights you should be running in the opposite direction from me, my lord. I have not set the best record for my behaviour."

"Now none of that, my lady. No more melancholy on this fine afternoon. We are having an adventure, and then we are going to have cake. Nothing could be more delightful."

His comical tone was just the thing to put a smile back on his companion's face, and they were both smiling as they clattered into the town of Uxbridge. Wesley had to pay closer attention to his team of horses, but he could see from the corner of his eye that Anne was gazing about with intelligent interest. He pulled up in front of the saddest looking hostelry in the village. All of a sudden, he was questioning the wisdom of bringing her here when he spotted the unsavoury characters watching their approach.

Her inquisitive glance at his hesitation prodded him into lifting her down from the carriage. It was too late to back out from this plan now. He just hoped it was early enough in the day that the men were not too far into their cups to be troublesome.

She must have picked up on his disquiet as she tucked her hand firmly into his elbow and kept close to his side as they entered the low establishment. The host approached them instantly.

"Good afternoon, my lord, what a pleasure to have you and your lady grace us with your presence." The obsequious man bowed and scraped before them.

Anne shrank back even closer to Wesley's side but did not make a sound. A quick glance in her direction showed Wesley that she was maintaining control over her features and only mild interest was displayed on her face despite the tight grip she had on his arm.

Wesley was surprised by a feeling of pride in her as though she were his protégé. He acknowledged that for the moment she was under his protection, but then sternly drew his attention back to the matter at hand. In order to properly protect the lady, he would need all his wits about him.

"The lady and I are here for some information. I have it on good authority that you have the information we seek."

The landlord's eyes gleamed and he rubbed his hands together, no doubt greedily imagining the coins the fine gentleman would have to part with to gain the information he sought. Wesley gritted his teeth and accepted the situation for what it was. But he could see that Lady Anne was drawing the attention of the patrons at the bar and quickly asked the landlord, "Is there somewhere we might be able to discuss the matter more privately?"

This caused the seedy man to appear even more delighted, no doubt imagining that private information would carry an even higher cost. Wesley suppressed his sigh and followed the thug to what appeared to be what was once a parlour but was now merely an oversized storage room.

"Unless you want to book a bed chamber, this is the most private we're going to get, milor'. Now, what can I do for you and the little lady?"

Wesley was glad Anne did not react to the sneer sent her way, nor did she launch into speech. He answered the landlord calmly. "We are looking for our friend Manfred Austen. We heard he had travelled through this way, and we were wondering if you had seen him."

"Well now, milord, me patrons value their privacy. I'm not so sure I should be sharing any such information with you. Perhaps this Manfred fellow isn't looking to be found."

Wesley clenched his fist in an effort to restrain himself from planting the man a facer. It would not do to resort to violence at this point, he reminded himself, especially not in front of a lady. But, oh, it was a challenge to stand there and not bruise up the man's already ugly face. No doubt others had been in the same predicament as he was but had been unable to restrain themselves. This thought brought him sufficient amusement to be able to calm down his ire for the moment.

He glanced down at his companion and could see from the bloom of colour on her cheeks that she was in full agreement with him in thinking the small man a buffoon. Wesley sighed and flipped a coin into the landlord's suddenly outstretched hand.

"Well now, milord, there did be someone calling themselves Manfred that passed through me fine establishment a couple days past. But I cannot say for certain if he be the very one you be looking for, now can I? Did you have a proper description of the fellow?"

Anne finally spoke up, which was a bit of a relief for Wesley as he couldn't rightly recall what her father looked like. He was pretty sure he would have been able to pick him out of a crowd, but to describe him, he would have been nonplussed. Wesley recalled Lord Austen as being the most nondescript person he had ever seen. But his daughter clearly had a different opinion. Wesley had to blink over the lengthy list of attributes she shared.

"He is this tall." She gestured with her hand, showing him to be about half a head taller than her. "His hair is the colour of gingerbread, and his eyes are pretty much the exact same colour. He has a small gap between his two front teeth and a small mole on his left cheekbone. His hair has a tendency to stick up in the front of his forehead because of a funny growth pattern he has. His father always says it was because a cow licked him when he was a lad." Wesley could hear her voice wobble on these last words, but she quickly gathered herself and carried on. "He was most likely wearing green, as that is his favourite colour, and he would wear it every single day if I did not prevent it."

The landlord was looking at her in amazement. "That is the most detailed description of another person I've ever heard. Are you his wife?"

"No!" Anne declared hotly. "He is my father."

"Ah! That explains it for sure. Well, then, yes, madam, he was here three days ago. He seemed to be a little dejected but in fine health. I don't think youse need to be worried about him none."

Wesley stepped into the conversation once more. "Did he happen to mention where he was going after he left your, uh, fine establishment?"

The landlord didn't seem to notice his hesitation and preened over Wesley's words. "I couldn't say for sure where he is right now, but I do know that he hitched a ride with Ben Downs when he was heading out of town. Maybe the other fellers at the bar know where Ben was heading." The sleazy landlord eyed them for a moment before offering. "Why don't you two sit here for a moment and I'll go ask the fellers."

Wesley nodded and the man left them on their own. Anne had not yet let go of his arm, and the viscount wondered if she had even forgotten that she was doing so. He patted her hand, wondering if she were in need of reassurance. Her nervous laughter answered his unasked question, and she quickly unwrapped her hands from around his elbow.

"I do apologize, my lord. I hope I have not caused your arm to go quite numb. I have a feeling my father would have apoplexy if he was to find out I had set foot in this place. Perhaps this was not the very best idea."

"No need to apologize, my lady. It is rather I who should be apologizing to you for bringing you here. I had not realized from the Runner's description that it was quite this low."

Anne giggled over his words. "Now, now, my lord, have you forgotten that this is a fine establishment? You did say so yourself."

Wesley grinned, appreciating that she was able to maintain her sense of humour despite the discomfort she was obviously feeling over being here.

"I do hope he returns quickly, my lord. I am feeling quite ready for that cup of tea you promised me."

He couldn't resist reaching out and tweaking her curls as they lay so fetchingly on her shoulder. "You, my dear, are the one who is being the jester now."

Before they could dissolve into hilarity, the landlord strode in. "You are a lucky devil, milord. The fellers recalled that Ben was headed to Wycombe, and they's pretty sure your friend Manfred went with him."

Wesley flipped the man another coin, grabbed Anne's hand, and headed out the door while calling out, "Thank you, my good man."

Once they had regained the street, Wesley slowed his pace, allowing Anne to come by his side. "I do believe from now on we shall leave this search firmly in the Runner's hands. What do you say?"

"That would probably be best." Anne's tone was hesitant.

"Why do you sound like that?"

She offered him a slight shrug. "While that was not the best location for a debutante, I have to say, it feels good to feel like I'm doing something to find my father. It is anticlimactic to leave it completely in someone else's hands. So, while I know you're probably right, and the Runner will be more successful more quickly, it is still a trifle disappointing."

"I appreciate your honesty, my lady. I will ensure the Runner reports to us as regularly as possible. Hopefully we will have you reunited with your father before many more days have passed."

Anne was looking at him with glowing eyes as she said a heartfelt, "Thank you, my lord," but then her face changed and she quirked her eyebrows at him. "Did you think to check on our estate, just in case he did just return home as you had suggested?"

Wesley had to laugh. "I did, actually. That was the first place I had him go."

"Of course, my lord. I should have known you would think of everything."

Again, Wesley felt himself puffing up with pride over her obvious admiration. He had no response for her words, so he merely guided her along to the much more acceptable George Inn where they were quickly welcomed by a nattily dressed landlord who bowed discretely and asked if they would require a private dining room or if the common room would be acceptable.

"There are no coaches expected this afternoon, my lord, and it is currently empty, so there is little chance of your lady being accosted."

"Thank you, Henry, that should be fine." Wesley could see that Anne was pondering the appropriateness of the situation, but she accepted his words and followed the landlord as he led them to a table. The landlord quickly bowed himself away with the promise to return promptly with their tea.

Once they were alone, Anne charmed him by leaning forward and whispering her question: "Promise me you will not think me completely ill-bred if I gaze around the room like a country bumpkin. It is doubtful my aunt will ever let me out on my own if she ever finds out where we have been this afternoon, so I wish to take full advantage while I have the chance." She didn't wait for his response but suited her words to actions, much to Wesley's amusement.

Ever a lady, she did manage not to allow her mouth to drop open, but she did display a surprising amount of fascination as she looked around the room. Before long, she brought her intelligent gaze back to meet Wesley's. There was a furrow of confusion between her brows.

"Can you explain to me why my aunt would have a fit of the vapours if she found out I was here? It doesn't actually look much different than Gunther's."

Wesley grinned over her question but then tried to explain it to her. "It is not the actual location your aunt is likely to have a problem with, but rather the possibility of associating with less than desirable fellow patrons. That is why Henry was quick to explain that there was no one else here."

Anne still looked dubious but nodded at his words. "That does sound plausible, my lord." She paused and glanced around the room again before continuing. "While this seems to be fine to me, it is probably best if we only tell my aunt about our drive, not about any of the stops we have made."

Wesley appreciated that his companion was not being overly high in the instep. He smiled at her but forbore to comment, as Henry was returning with a laden tray.

With a flourish, their host served them each delectable looking pastries and poured them steaming hot tea. When he asked if they needed anything else, Wesley waved him away.

Anne's sigh was not of the melancholy variety after she swallowed her first bite. She politely placed her fork back onto her plate before she grinned at Wesley. "This right here, my lord, is why I need to marry a gentleman of means. After the delectable treats I have been enjoying since being in London, I do not know if I could bear to return to Rowanwood and our housekeeper's less than stellar cookery." She paused, looking sheepish. "I suppose I shouldn't blame her. I don't know how to bake such delicious things either." She took another delicate bite, her expression pensive. "Actually, my lord, now that I think on it, I really ought not to place this solution in finding a husband. There is nothing to say that I cannot learn how to bake my own treats, is there? And surely my father would enjoy it, too."

"Are you changing your mind about our plan?" Wesley questioned, surprised.

Tilting her head and looking him straight in the eye, Anne answered. "I am trying to keep my options open, my lord. I think I am beginning to realize I would rather be happy than wealthy if I am forced to choose. And these pastries make me happy."

Wesley returned her grin, but inside he was thinking his respect for the chit was rapidly increasing. "I am glad you are enjoying the treat."

As they were finishing the last of their cakes, in the distance a clock could be heard sounding the hour.

"Oh dear, is it really that late?" Anne asked. "My aunt is going to be beside herself if I am not home soon, as we are promised to the Wickshams' and the Roxboroughs' tonight."

"Two balls, my lady? You are going to be quite worn out on the morrow."

Anne's trill of laughter answered his observation. "Is it not every debutante's dream, my lord?"

"Probably." He smiled back at her while helping her to her feet. Wesley quickly settled with Henry and ushered Anne back out into the sunshine. "Have no fear, my lady, I shall return you to Town as quickly as possible. Your aunt shall have no reason to ring a peal over you if I can help it."

"Do not trouble yourself too much, my lord. Despite my warnings, she is no doubt sitting in her withdrawing room planning our wedding breakfast as we speak."

Wesley joined her in laughter but was amazed he did not feel a shudder of revulsion at her words. Perhaps it was time to allow his friends to take over escorting her. It would not do to let himself develop any feelings for the chit. He was most definitely not finished with his single days.

Chapter Seven

Within minutes, they were rolling along the road back to London, setting a brisk pace that was eating up the miles.

Anne was pensive, trying to identify the emotion she was feeling. It had been a long time since she had experienced it. She suspected it might be contentment.

She turned to the viscount, surprised that he had been quiet for so long. She frowned when she saw the disturbed expression on his face. "Is something troubling you, my lord?"

"As a matter of fact, yes," he replied. When she merely looked at him with raised eyebrows, he continued, "I think you should make clear to your aunt that even if you were to catch me in a compromising situation, I would suppress the gentleman in me and refuse to do what most would consider the honourable thing. I am not such a fool as the Earl of Heath."

Anne felt as though he had struck her with that statement. She felt the colour ebbing and flowing in her face but could not come up with a suitable reply to his uncalled for statement. She willed the tears she felt gathering in her eyes not to fall. She did not want to give him the satisfaction of knowing he had hurt her, as she was certain that had been his aim.

"From what I heard, the earl and countess have found joy with one another, but I will be sure to tell my aunt your feelings on the subject," she answered him, trying not to sound too sarcastic. There was a lengthening silence as she contemplated his words further. "It does strike me as rather strange that you would escort me on this errand if you were in fear of me trying to entrap you into marriage, my lord."

Her stilted tone must have finally gotten through to the viscount as he quickly set about trying to reassure her. "No, no, my lady, I can assure you, I am not actually in fear of you trying such a stunt. I know full well that you backed out of doing it even with the duke, but I think you should ensure your aunt understands that such a ploy would not work with me, just in case she is of a similar mind as your father."

Anne looked at the viscount, mortified. "Do you actually think I won't be able to find a husband without trapping him? What do you consider to be so horrible about me that no one will want me?"

She could see that the viscount was suitably horrified at the direction this conversation was heading, but she did not care to spare his feelings.

"I am truly sorry, Lady Anne. I did not mean to so insult you. It was just your comment about your aunt planning our nuptials that set me on edge. Clearly, I spoke without thought. I beg of you to forgive me for being so mutton headed."

Anne was not fully mollified, but she could not help the watery chuckle that his words prompted. "I can assure you, I have no wish for an unwilling groom, nor am I about to try to change your mind. But might I ask why you are so dead set against marriage?"

"I am not actually so opposed to it in theory. In fact, I know that someday I will have to settle down and become leg shackled. I would even go so far as to say if I had met you five years from now I would be much more interested in your aunt's schemes. But I have not yet finished enjoying my life as a bachelor, and I will not allow anyone to hurry me in that direction."

"That is fine, my lord. I doubt I would want to be leg shackled to an overbearing rake such as yourself with an overinflated opinion of his own importance. I have every intention of finding a nice quiet gentleman who is anxious to settle down to a quiet life with me. I have no desire to have to drag someone to the altar."

Anne could feel the viscount's discomfort with the turn the afternoon had taken, but she was too disappointed herself to be able to smooth it over just at the moment. She felt as though her foundations were once again being shaken. It reaffirmed her conviction that she had no one to rely on except herself. Melancholy swamped her for a moment, but she allowed herself to relax and enjoy the scenery.

Within a few minutes, she was able to pull herself back from despair and before they had travelled a couple of miles, she had allowed the familiar scenery to lull her back into a more comfortable feeling. Finally she felt ready to resume conversing with the viscount.

"Have you been to the theatre yet this Season, my lord?"

He appeared surprised by her question but quickly responded. "I have, yes, a time or two. It is not my very favourite activity, but it can be a pleasant way to pass the evening. What about you, my lady? Have you been to the theatre often?"

"I have never been. My aunt does not have a box, and I have not yet been invited to join someone else in theirs. But I think I would enjoy the experience if I get to go sometime. Why is it not your favourite?"

"The audience can be unbelievably rude. I think the players on stage have probably put a great deal of effort into preparing their parts and yet most cannot be bothered to even watch."

"Not watch? Whatever do you mean? Surely that is the point of going to the theatre, is it not?" Anne was unsure if he were jesting with her.

"I can understand why you would think so, but no, it does not seem that the wellborn consider the actual production to be worthy of their attention. It seems the majority attend the theatre merely to watch each other."

Anne had to laugh over his words. "Well then, it is not unlike any other event of the Season, my lord. But it does seem a shame. And I still think I would like to see it for myself."

"I shall arrange for a box and make a group so that you can attend. Would sometime next week work for you, do you think? Or have you already accepted invitations for every evening?"

Anne frowned, not at his words, but at the way her unreasonable heart seemed to skip a beat at his words. She admonished herself not to be a widgeon and quickly answered the viscount. "I would not want to put you to any more trouble than you have already done for me, my lord. That would be too kind of you."

"I strongly doubt there is such a thing as too kind, my dear. And it is no trouble. It is not as though I dislike the theatre, just the other patrons. And I will ensure that I like everyone in my box, so it shan't be a trial at all."

Anne was doubtful over his words but was so anxious to go that she decided not to quibble. "Well, if you are sure, my lord, I will not be missish about it but will readily admit that I would be delighted if you could arrange it and include me. You would probably have to include my aunt in the invitation, unless you have some other equally acceptable matron that you could include."

"Leave that all with me," he assured her. "I will make sure it is highly acceptable. But you didn't say if you are engaged for every evening."

"I do not think we have yet accepted invitations for most of next week. My aunt likes to wait and see if we get any better offers." Anne felt the heat creeping once again into her cheeks. "Does that not seem rude, my lord? I feel badly for the hostesses who are waiting to know their numbers."

"Your aunt is certainly not the only one with such a tactic. It is expected, I am sure, especially of the debutantes. I think the older ladies are more set on which entertainments they wish to attend and do not need to be wishy washy about it."

Anne wrinkled her nose as she pondered his words. "So, you do not think we are putting anyone out overly?"

"I very much doubt it. As you know, most of the events you attend are crowded nearly to the point of excess. It seems unlikely the hostess would be too put out if a debutante or two chose to go elsewhere."

"You are most likely correct. It's not as though the debutantes are all that important anyway, is it?"

"That is where I would have to disagree with you. The debutantes are almost the entire reason for the whole farce, don't you think? The rest of the *ton* entertains themselves by watching as the debutantes make their curtsy to Society and go about the business of contracting a husband. Do you realize there are even betting books set up in the clubs over the results of the Season?"

Anne was horrified. "Surely you are jesting, my lord. That seems terribly ill bred."

"It may be ill bred, but that does not mean it is not true," he pointed out.

"Are you placing bets on it?" she asked, curious, before she almost shrilled, "Am I in there?"

She almost flinched when he reached over to pat her hand, no doubt trying to offer her comfort. "Do not get in a taking, my dear. I do not stoop to such bets. I have not looked at the lists, and I have not heard anyone bandying your name about, but it is most likely that you are on the books as you have made your debut this Season."

"How vulgar," was all she could think to say. She subsided into thought for a moment before she had an idea and started to chuckle.

"What have you found to amuse you now?" the viscount demanded.

"It might be a way for my father to straighten out his finances," she giggled.

She recognized the incredulous expression on the viscount's face before he joined her in laughter. "You, my dear, are a bang up girl. You had sounded so thoroughly horrified at the thought of anyone taking bets over your marital prospects, but now that you see a way to benefit from it, you think your father should participate. Was it not gambling that led him into the trouble he finds himself in in the first place?"

"I never said it was a good idea, just that it was an idea," she protested. "You are absolutely right. It would be a horrible idea, besides being unethical since we could control the outcome. Hardly seems sporting, does it?"

The viscount was still chuckling and shook his head at her words. "I am undecided if you are slightly touched in your upper works or if you are the most amazing girl I have ever had the pleasure of meeting."

Anne offered him a cheeky grin. "No doubt a little bit of both."

She was delighted that she had managed to hide from him the depth of her hurt and that they were managing to maintain their camaraderie. Anne did enjoy the viscount's company but reminded herself to be on guard not to entrust him with her feelings in the future.

Despite their return to comfortable companionship, Anne was relieved when they clattered back onto her street and the viscount handed her down from his carriage in front of her aunt's house.

"Save me a dance at the Roxborough ball, my lady. I might be a trifle late, as I have a few things I need to do before turning up there, but I promise I shall put in an appearance."

Anne couldn't decide how she felt about his words. "As you could see this morning, you have already accomplished what you set out to do for me, so you need not trouble yourself about my popularity, my lord."

"It does not trouble me, my dear, but I now feel responsible for you, and I want to be there to ensure you are being properly treated."

She lifted her eyebrows at him but refrained from further comment. Dipping into a curtsy, she thanked him for the afternoon and hurried up the stairs.

"Good afternoon, my lady, did you have a good drive? Your aunt was just wondering about you." Anne looked at the butler anxiously to try to gage his words, but he did not seem like he was suppressing his thoughts, so she didn't think she needed to be overly concerned about her aunt's reaction. The viscount had been true to his word and made rapid progress returning to Town. But she ought to look in on her aunt and make sure everything was all right.

"Where might I find her ladyship?" she asked.

"I believe she is in her retiring room, my lady."

"Thank you." She hurried off to see what her aunt was doing.

"Oh, Anne, how lovely that you are home. I was just beginning to wonder if I should be worried." She glanced quickly at the clock on the mantle. "But you have made it just in time not to have to rush in your preparations for this evening. It is a good thing we have not been invited anywhere for supper, though," she concluded on a reproving tone.

"I would have made certain to be back before now if we had been," Anne assured her aunt, trying not to be frustrated. "Have you had a pleasant afternoon?"

"Quite, yes, thank you for asking. Now run along and get ready. Sally should be already waiting for you in your room."

"Thank you, my lady." Anne curtsied and made her way out of the room. She need not have worried about her aunt's reaction to her absence. It did not seem that her ladyship was at all concerned with where she had been all afternoon.

Climbing the stairs to her room, Anne contemplated the evening to come. She was quite ready to be finished with the Season as it was not turning out to be to her taste. Hopefully she would be able to come up with a plan that would allow her to not require a husband or else she would find a suitable match within the coming days as she was quite ready to go back to the country.

Sally greeted her with warm enthusiasm. "How was your drive with the viscount, my lady? I did not think you would be quite so long. I do hope you didn't run into any difficulties while you were out."

"Thank you for asking, Sally." Anne smiled at her maid. "It was a lovely afternoon. We drove rather further than I had expected, which is why we were a little long, but it was so nice to get outside of the city for a time."

The maid sighed. "Oh, I can imagine."

Anne's ready sympathy came to the fore. "Are you feeling homesick, Sally?"

The maid blushed hotly. "Oh, never mind about me, my lady. Her ladyship would not want to hear about me pining."

"I shan't say a word to my aunt, Sally, have no fear. But it would be perfectly understandable if you were longing for the country. You grew up on my uncle's estate, did you not?"

"Yes, the cook there is me mum."

"Well then, of course you would long to be there. I do not blame you. While there are lovely parts to being in the city, for the most it is just not the right way to live. We should have fields and forests and animals all around rather than rows and rows of houses and shops and factories. This just isn't natural in my opinion."

Sally giggled over Anne's words but couldn't argue with them. "But surely you are enjoying yourself here, though, aren't you, milady? Going to balls and such must be lovely."

Anne was suddenly struck with guilt. While she was lamenting, it was really playtime for her, whereas the maid was working constantly to make it all possible.

"Of course it is lovely, and I have you to thank for making it so."

"Now get on with you, my lady, it is all your aunt's doing."

"She is not the one who dresses my hair and presses my gowns. If I was not presentable, I can assure you I would not be having a good time."

The maid couldn't argue with Anne's logic, so she merely giggled and got on with the business of preparing her lady for the evening.

They were suddenly interrupted by the arrival of Anne's bath. Before long there was a full tub of steaming water and Anne sank in and allowed her worries to wash away.

It didn't take too long before she was ready for the ball. A footman had delivered a tray of food for her to enjoy rather than taking the time for a proper meal in the dining room, since they were all going out that evening. Anne was relieved she would not have to try to make conversation until later. Glancing at her reflection before heading out the door, she was surprised to see that she looked rather well. Once again she would not be the homeliest girl in attendance, for which fact she would be eternally grateful. She wasn't sure what it was, but her adventures with the Viscount of Bracondale seemed to be agreeing with her despite the danger to her heart. She braced her shoulders and prepared to face another ball.

Chapter Eight

The ball was just getting into full swing when they arrived. Anne was happy to see that it was not yet a crush when she and her aunt and uncle were announced. For the first time, her name produced a tiny reaction amongst the assembled crowd. A shiver ran down Anne's back. She was undecided if it were better to be completely anonymous or to be a person of interest. She could not even imagine how the Diamonds of the Season could bear all the attention they received. Maybe they considered it their due.

She was rather distracted with her thoughts as she gained the ballroom and did not notice the Earl of Sutton approaching until he was right in front of her.

"My lady," he greeted her with more enthusiasm than she had received from him the previous night, much to her surprise.

"Good evening, my lord," she returned his greeting, dipping into a curtsy.

"You are looking lovely," he complimented after looking her over thoroughly.

She felt her cheeks warm but was not overly embarrassed. His inspection had been of the detached variety, as though he were checking her for defects, as if she were a horse at Tattersall's or something. For some indiscernible reason this struck her as amusing rather than offensive. She examined him but knew she would not be able to imitate his manner so refrained from trying. She returned the compliment. "As do you, my lord. I quite fancy the interesting manner in which you have tied your neck cloth this evening."

The earl appeared surprised by her words, and Anne was amazed to see a splash of colour cover his cheekbones for a moment. "Why thank you for noticing, my dear. I have no wish to be a dandy, but I do make an effort to turn myself out to advantage when I am attending this sort of thing."

"I would say you achieved your aim."

"You are a rather strange girl, aren't you, my lady?" he asked her quizzically, making her choke on a gurgle of laughter.

"I do not know what to say to that, my lord."

"Of course you don't. Forgive my foolishness. I allowed words to leave my mouth before my mind was fully engaged. It was meant to be a compliment, although I realize it did not sound like it. I meant that you are not like the other debutantes, always wishing to discuss themselves. You actually seem to have some interesting thoughts in your head, which makes it a relief to spend some time with you."

"Why, Lord Spencer, that is quite the nicest thing anyone has said to me."

Again colour splashed onto his cheeks and he looked uncomfortable for the briefest moment, but then it vanished and he was the perfectly composed earl as usual. Bowing over her hand, he asked, "Might I have the pleasure of this dance? It sounds to me as though it is a minuet."

Anne curtsied and accepted, and he swept her onto the dance floor with the other assembling couples. Since the earl was a skilled dance partner, Anne enjoyed her time with him, but she was not disappointed when they left the dance floor and another gentleman was waiting for an introduction. The earl performed that duty.

"My lady, allow me to present to you Lord Matthew Seymour, the Baron of Walmsley. Walmsley, this is Lady Anne Austen."

Lord Seymour bowed over Anne's hand politely but without undue flourishing, which she quite liked. "It is a pleasure to make your acquaintance, my lady. Might I have the pleasure of sharing this next dance with you?"

Anne accepted and followed him onto the dance floor. It was a country dance, so they were unable to converse very much, but she was able to find out that Walmsley was not too awfully far from Rowanwood, a little fact that she took to be a positive sign.

When the dance came to an end, rather than offering to escort her to her aunt, the baron asked if he might take her to the refreshment table for a glass of punch. Anne took that as another point in his favour if he were wishing to spend a little more time with her rather than just being gallant in offering to procure her refreshment. She accepted, placing her hand into his elbow.

"Have you been in Town long, my lady?" he asked.

"My father and I arrived almost three weeks ago. What about you?"

"My mother and I just arrived two days ago. I was a little late with the harvest this year and did not want to leave our estate until everything was fully sorted. I must tell you, these Society affairs are not my favourite way to spend time, but my mother wished to come and felt unable to do so without my escort, so here we are."

"It is good of you to see to her comforts," Anne thought to say, wondering if he were perhaps a trifle too attached to his mother.

"She just got out of her mourning, so it would have been her first time to travel alone," he explained.

"Oh, I am sorry for your loss."

The baron grinned. "She was not mourning for my father. I wasn't overly attached to her second husband, so your sympathies are misplaced, my lady. She isn't even all that old yet, so she is thinking to find herself husband number three, which is why she was so disgruntled with me for not getting her here for the very beginning of the Season."

Anne couldn't help but laugh lightly over his choice of words. "You could point out to her that since the Season is already under way, now that she is newly arrived, she will have the advantage of being a novelty. Everyone else has already met each other. She might be more interesting for being new."

"You are a clever minx, aren't you?"

Not sure how to take his words, Anne merely smiled and took another sip of her punch, pleased to find that it was actually rather tasty.

"So what is your story, Lady Anne? Are you an heiress just here to enjoy the ball, or are you, like my mother, also on the hunt for a husband?"

Anne blinked at him and tried not to allow her mouth to drop open at his unusual question. He hurried to explain himself.

"I would rather hear it from you than have to ask my mother what she might know about you."

She again had to bite back her laughter at his words. "I guess I appreciate your honesty in that case, my lord. I will be honest with you in return. I am the only daughter of an impoverished viscount who hasn't a sixpence to scratch with, as the footman would say."

Now the baron laughed at her word choice. "I like your spunk, my lady."

Anne blushed over his words. She would never have thought anyone would describe her in such terms. She was just a country mouse. But she liked that he thought otherwise.

The baron lifted his head and gazed about the room. "I can see that your attention is about to be seized from me, my lady. Would it be acceptable to you if I called on you tomorrow?"

A small thrill ran through Anne. She might have finally found the gentleman who could be the perfect husband. She smiled and nodded. "I would like that, my lord," she said shyly.

"Lady Anne!"

Anne turned abruptly at Lord Sebastian Grey's hearty address. "Good evening, my lord," she answered in a more demure tone.

"You are looking ravishing, my lady. I was hoping to share the next dance with you. It is not at all the thing to allow this bumpkin to monopolize all of your time this evening."

She almost gasped at Lord Grey's inflammatory words but was relieved when the baron merely chuckled. "Imagine my amazement that Lady Roxborough has seen fit to allow the likes of you to attend her fancy ball."

Anne was all the more confused when the two gentlemen shook hands heartily before Lord Grey offered Anne his elbow.

"Shall we proceed?" he asked.

"That would be lovely," she stammered.

They walked in silence together toward the ballroom, and Anne noticed it was to be a waltz. She was unsure how she would be able to face the nobleman after his earlier words.

Lord Grey chuckled low in Anne's ear. "You look slightly horrified still, my dear. Do try not to judge me too harshly. The baron and I have known one another since we were youngsters. We are actually cousins of a sort, if you scrutinize the family tree closely enough."

"Is that how gentlemen usually greet one another?" she asked, fascinated.

"Often, when they have that sort of long-standing relationship. I am sure women are much different, but men enjoy that sort of thing."

"I guess I shall have a lot to learn if I ever get married, won't I?"

"That you will, my dear," he agreed heartily. "But do not allow it to trouble you. My friends and I shall make sure you are matched with someone who will never give you cause for concern."

"That is such a charming promise, my lord, thank you." Even if she didn't fully believe him, it was kind of him to say.

She allowed a pause to follow, and they circled the room in silence for a moment before she asked what was on her mind. "What do you really think of Lord Seymour?"

Lord Grey chuckled over her question but gave it serious thought before he answered her. "I actually quite respect the man he grew up to be, even though he was a bit of a clunch when we were boys. He's merely a baron and his lands are not extensive, but they include mines so he is far from a pauper. He has his mother on his hands now since her second husband passed away, but rumour has it she's on the prowl for another one, so that shouldn't be too much of a concern. You could do far worse, my lady," was his eventual conclusion.

Anne felt the colour rising in her cheeks over the audacity of having this conversation with a gentleman unrelated to her. He laughed over her discomfort just as their dance was coming to an end. "Now don't go getting all missish on me now, my lady. We have decided to be friends, have we not? Is this not the type of thing you would discuss with your friends?"

She couldn't help laughing. "It is still highly questionable, my lord, but let us leave it at that. Thank you for the dance."

"It was entirely my pleasure," Lord Grey replied as he bowed over her hand, kissing her wrist.

Anne watched dispassionately, surprised that she didn't get goose bumps over his gallantry. Perhaps she was growing immune, she thought, curious. The couple times Lord Dunbar had done the same thing she had felt the thrill all the way to her toes. She wondered if it were possible for the novelty to wear off so quickly.

As if her thoughts had conjured him, when she turned around the viscount was there with his crooked smile, waiting to claim her for the next dance. She was glad the waltz had just played so it was unlikely the next one would be another. She was determined not to allow the viscount to turn her head or her heart.

She curtsied her acceptance of his invitation to dance, and he swept her into the minuet. It was a relief that it separated them much of the time, so there was little opportunity for conversation. She could even avoid meeting his eyes as she gazed about the room and at the other dancers. She was quite certain she had managed to avoid anything uncomfortable and yet still be polite with him. But when she finally did meet his eyes, she realized she had not been as successful as she might have wished. The searching look he gave her made her realize he was going to be asking her some awkward questions at his earliest opportunity. She looked around frantically, hoping to avoid it. She couldn't help smiling in delight as she saw Lord Seymour waiting for her when the dance was over.

She thanked Lord Dunbar as prettily as she could muster and then quickly turned to the baron. He bowed to her. "That looked lovely, my lady. Might I have the pleasure once more?"

He calmly waited for her reply unlike the viscount who had assumed her acceptance and swept her onto the dance floor as he was asking. Anne assured herself that Lord Seymour's manner was far more desirable.

This next song was a country dance. She was relieved because at the moment she had no idea what she could possibly talk about with anyone. She hated the thought of making small talk. There was really only so much you could say about the weather, and she couldn't bear all the gossip everyone always seemed to wish to discuss. Of course, she could always attempt to get to know the man better, she reminded herself in amusement. Anne was surprised to see the baron's eyes light up when he saw her smile as the dance brought them back together.

"You seem to be having a good time, my lady," he commented.

There was no way she could explain the thought process that had led to her smile, so she merely smiled and nodded in return. Following through on her thought, she asked him, "Are you enjoying your evening, my lord?"

"I am now," he said, his significant look leading her to believe he meant now that he had met her. She could feel the heat rising in her cheeks over his words. Uncertain, she returned his smile with a small one of her own.

The dance separated them again, much to Anne's relief. While this was the very purpose of these events, now that she found herself facing the very real possibility of a gentleman showing a marked interest in her, she didn't quite know what to make of it. She really needed to get to know him better!

When the dance brought them back together again, she was ready.

"Have you escorted your mother here this evening?"

"Yes, I have, would you like to meet her?"

He sounded so eager, but that had not been Anne's intention when she asked. There was nothing she could say except, "Of course, I would love to meet her." She hated untruths but under the circumstances there was no other possible answer.

When the dance ended, the baron escorted her to the side of the room where a group of older ladies were sitting with their heads together.

"Mother, I would like to introduce you to someone, if I could have your attention for a moment."

Anne thought she would sink to the floor with mortification as three pairs of eyes turned to them with incredulous expressions. She dipped into a respectful curtsy, unsure who any of the women were but certain from their haughty faces that they were quite convinced of their own importance. She wondered if the baron was oblivious or cruel as she struggled to keep a pleasant and polite smile on her face.

"Good evening." The lady in the middle finally spoke after staring at her almost insolently for a full minute.

Anne stepped forward to shake her hand as she dipped into another curtsy. "My lady, it is a pleasure to meet you."

"This is Lady Anne Austen, Mother. Lady Anne, my mother, Lady Halstead."

Lady Halstead offered her son a brilliant smile as she introduced her two cronies to him.

"My dear boy, I am sure you have heard me mention my dear friends, Lady Ruttledge and Lady Glenn. We have been having the most delightful evening catching up on each other's news. I am glad to see you are having a good evening, as well. But I am certain your young friend has no wish to sit amongst us old ladies, so why don't you be a good boy and fetch the three of us some punch?"

Anne was not disappointed to be dismissed so quickly. It really had not been an appropriate time for the baron to introduce her to his mother. But the lady had not turned out to be a total shrew, so perhaps they could salvage the situation at some other time.

As they walked away, the baron must have realized the error he had made. "I do apologize, my lady. I should have realized my mother would be too occupied with her friends to wish to make new acquaintances this evening. Perhaps we could call on you some time."

"I am sure that would be lovely. Anne wasn't sure if she was being fully truthful but was willing to give it another try.

"I had best see to their punch," Lord Seymour was saying, looking harried all of a sudden.

Anne smiled, releasing him. "It has been a pleasure, my lord. I see my aunt over there. Perhaps I shall join her."

She had no desire to do so, but hoped to find a distraction along the way, so she happily left the baron to his errand. Her wish was granted as another gentleman asked for her hand and she was swept into the next waltz.

By the time she was tucked into her bed that night by Sally, Anne had nearly danced a hole in the soles of her dancing slippers and she was well satisfied with the success of her Season. She did hope her father would turn up before too long. She would have a great deal to discuss with him when she finally saw him.

Chapter Nine

Kate & Austen:

Austen stretched his aching back as he looked along the row of stalls. He had never worked so hard in all his life. He strongly doubted a doctor would approve of him working like this after the beating he had taken, but he found he was more content than he had been in ages, maybe ever. He never would have thought that hard work would lead to such a feeling, but there was the proof right in front of him. He thought with a grin of what his daughter would think if she were to lay eyes on him at this moment.

Kate chose that moment to walk up to him. She returned his grin with one of her own, which caused a small flutter in the area of his chest. Austen chose to ignore the sensation.

"Good afternoon, Mrs. Appleton," he greeted her.

"I think it is safe for you to call me Kate, my lord, since you are a nobleman who happens to be mucking out my stalls."

Austen grinned at her again. "You should call me Austen, then. It's what my friends used to call me."

"What do they call you now?" she asked, obviously curious.

Heat crept into his cheeks as he realized he should have curbed his tongue. He didn't want to admit to her that he no longer had any friends, so he attempted to change the subject.

"Your foreman is a slave driver, Kate."

She smiled. "You probably should be still in bed after what you have been through."

"Oh, please, don't chase me back indoors," he wheedled. "I haven't found anything this diverting in years."

"You have led a strange and sad life, my lord, Austen, if you find mucking out the stalls to be a good time."

He shrugged. There was no arguing with her logic. It was the satisfaction of accomplishment, not the actual activity, that was leaving him feeling so refreshed. It would be too long of a story to try to explain. "Do you know what my next task is to be?"

"I do believe you have earned some nourishment. Come along with me. The cook has sent you a picnic."

"Oh how lovely, thank you. I surely couldn't come in the house in this state." He made quick work of washing his hands and face in the trough then followed in her wake as she led him to a bench situated near the house.

"Are you quite certain you are not over doing yourself with all this work?" Kate asked, her tone a little anxious.

"I have so much to learn and cannot presume upon your hospitality much longer. I cannot be sitting about when I have this great opportunity presented to me."

"You are not burdening us with your presence here, in fact, it is a pleasure to have a new person to talk to."

They munched on their lunch for a few minutes in silence as Austen digested her words. He was deeply grateful and had no desire to take advantage. He was long overdue on getting his life on track. He needed to do this for himself and his daughter.

"I really ought to send a message to my daughter. She is probably beginning to get a bit worried that she has not heard from me."

"You may make use of my library whenever you wish." She paused for a moment in thought. "Actually, I think you might need to learn a little bit about record keeping, so if you would like, I could show you that this afternoon. It will keep you away from my steward for a little while and give you some much needed instruction." She blushed fiercely at this and began to stammer. "Not to imply that I am a fit instructor, of course, or that you have been mistaken in something because I, of course, know nothing of the state of the books at your estate."

Austen laughed and broke into her disjointed speech. "I took no offense, Kate, let me assure you. You are quite right that I know nothing about record keeping. But how could you have known this?"

Her blush remained. "It is the first thing I thought of when you explained how straightened your circumstances have become. It is unlikely that a viscount's estate should get to such a state unless you are being swindled by someone, and it would show in the books. Do you have a steward that you trust?"

"I never thought about it, I am afraid. I have a steward. He has had ready explanations whenever I lamented the state of our coffers. Since I didn't know anything about it, I never thought to question him."

"Well, I can give you some ideas about what to look for," she told him.

"You know how to do these records?" Austen was even more ashamed of himself. If this lovely young woman was capable of doing it, surely he should have been able as well.

Austen thought she was about to say "of course," but then thought better of it. She simply nodded before explaining, "Since I was the only child, my father knew this would all be mine one day, so he made sure I knew how to look after it. Even though I married, he never wanted me to feel ignorant." She paused again, obviously uncomfortable with what she was about to ask. "Did your father not give you the same instruction?"

"Unfortunately, no." Austen looked out at the heartening view of Kate's thriving farm. "My father was even more dissolute than me." He found it in him to laugh. "I, at least, recognize that changes need to be made." Then more self-deprecatingly, he continued, "Of course, that could be just because I have hit the bottom, so there is no other choice."

She was looking at him with a serious, steady gaze. "I think there is always a choice, my lord. As you said, you could just rely on your daughter for an advantageous match. In fact, you aren't even that old. You could probably find an heiress to wed."

Austen shuddered at the suggestion. "Can you imagine? For any bourgeois father to be willing to give me his daughter and a large sum of money, he would have to be a very loose fish besides being a vulgar mushroom. And his daughter would have to be bracket-faced and bird-witted. No, thank you."

Kate burst into gales of laughter at his words. It took her a few minutes to get her mirth under control, and she had to wipe the tears from her eyes before she could look at him clearly. "I do not think it would be as bad as all that, but I can see your point, my lord. Very well, let us see if we can arrange it so you can get yourself sorted. Then you can carry on however you wish."

By the time they had finished discussing the matter they had also finished their meal, so they went inside to follow through on their plan. First though, Austen needed to change out of his work clothes. As he slowly climbed his way up to his room, he was glad Kate had thought to acquire a change of clothes for him from one of the stable hands, otherwise he would no longer be fit company. As quickly as he could, despite his aches and pains, he stripped off the offensive garments, cleaned himself up as best as he could without a valet's assistance, and changed back into his own clothes.

Despite his dread for the task ahead, as numbers were never his favourite while he was a boy, Austen was looking forward to the afternoon spent in Kate's company. She was such a kind young woman, he thought as he made his slow descent back down to where she was waiting patiently for him, her pleasant smile brightening up the room.

"Ready, my lord?"

"As ready as I am likely to ever be," he grumbled good naturedly as they made their way slowly to her library.

"You seem to have developed some new aches and pains for your efforts this morning," she commented, her mild tone belying the worried look on her face.

"Nothing that a good night's sleep shouldn't fix up. Do not trouble yourself, I beg of you."

She looked dubious but refrained from further comment. When they finally arrived, she stepped inside and Austen was able to see the welcoming room within. It was much like any library in countless country homes throughout the nation, he surmised, even not unlike his own at Rowanwood. But unlike his, this room had a welcoming, well-used air about it. As though you could make yourself at home in that room and be comfortable. If he had to face the task of learning how to read records, he doubted they could have found a more congenial location.

"This is a remarkable room, Kate. No wonder you don't mind your labours here. I might even find the task less than horrible in a room such as this."

Kate laughed and looked around at what was no doubt a familiar scene to the point of being oblivious to its power. "It took me a while to be comfortable in here, to be honest with you, Austen." She smiled shyly over her use of his name. "Since I associate this room so directly with my father, it took me weeks before I could even come in here without weeping. But now, the room and I have made peace with one another. I am delighted that you like it. I hope it makes our task less onerous for you."

Glancing around the room, her gaze settled on the table set in front of the large windows. "Why don't we sit there? It'll be far more comfortable than trying to crane our necks if we're across my desk from one another." She promptly ensured there were two chairs comfortably positioned, and she gathered up her records as well as some paper, a pen, and the inkwell from her desk.

Austen was once again swept with a sense of shame that this slip of a woman was waiting on him. She was not a servant, and he had no intention of treating her like one.

"Please, let me help you with that," he protested.

"Never mind, my lord, I can be much faster if I do it myself. Just find a comfortable position for yourself as we are likely to be here for a while."

He ceased his protests and took a seat. The chair she had indicated was remarkably comfortable despite being made of wood without any cushioning. He hoped he would be able to keep his attention on the matter at hand; he thought a less comfortable chair might be of more assistance in that regard. But as she said, if they were to be there for any length of time it would not do to add to his physical ailments.

They settled in and got to work. She explained the principles involved with keeping the household accounts and what sort of things he ought to look for when reviewing for errors. She then set him to the task of reviewing her records for any errors.

"But I doubt you would have any mistakes," he protested.

"You can never be too careful," she replied coyly at first before grinning and saying, "If you see what a proper ledger looks like, hopefully you will be in a good position to verify if yours are being kept properly. This is merely an exercise to get you used to the task, my lord. Do try not to over think the matter."

Austen sighed. "It is a difficult task to turn over a new leaf, Kate. Have mercy."

She just laughed and tapped the paper.

Before long, Austen found that it was not nearly as difficult as he had expected. While he had been a poor student, particularly in the field of mathematics, seeing the practical application of the dreaded subject made it much easier. He was almost enjoying himself. Of course, the company didn't hurt when it came to that.

Finally, when he came to the end of the column, he glanced up into her smiling face. "You are a godsend, my dear. It would be such a wondrous thing if I could take you home with me to Rowanwood and you could help me straighten out my messes there. With your tutelage here, it doesn't look so hard, but I think in the case of a mess like I have, it will be an impossible task for me."

He was surprised when she blushed to the roots of her hair and started to stammer out a reply. "Oh no, my lord, I am certain you shall be quite capable of managing without me. Despite the knock on your head, you are an apt pupil. Surely you shan't need me. Besides, you would soon tire of having a tutor."

Austen chuckled and did not pursue the subject at that moment, but the idea began to take root. She would be a perfect companion. Perhaps he could hire her as his steward, he thought, as he reflected on the idea of prolonging their association.

Kate turned the subject. "Did you wish to have a few minutes of privacy to compose your letter to your daughter, my lord, Austen?"

"You needn't leave for me to do that. I feel as though I have no secrets from you at this point." He grinned at her, fascinated by her shy smile.

"Well, I was planning to leave to get us some tea, but I won't bother prolonging the task if you don't mind my being here," she informed him.

"What is the complete opposite of minding?" he asked rhetorically. She departed the room, leaving behind her tinkling laughter and the faintest scent of lemons in her wake.

He stared at one of the blank pieces of paper she had left for him, pondering what he could say to his daughter, especially knowing she might not be the only one who read it. He finally pulled the paper a little closer to himself and set to his task.

My dearest Anne,

I trust this letter finds you well. Please accept my humblest apologies for leaving without a word. I needed to get away for a space and then ran into difficulties. I have made some new friends and am being well cared for at the moment. I hope to return to you in London within a few days.

Take care,

Father

He reread his words. There was no information contained in the missive, but it would assure his daughter that he was alive and well, which was the only purpose it served. There was no way to explain, even if he wanted to, to his daughter the complete change he felt coming over him, especially not in a letter. If he sensed she could handle it when he was with her again, he would make the attempt, but certainly not from this distance. What he had written would have to do. He sanded the letter and waited for Kate's return to request sealing wax.

"I hope I'm not interrupting," Kate declared as she entered the room, followed by a servant.

Austen found Kate's household to be run in a fascinating manner. It was obviously a thriving estate; she was clearly a woman of some means. But she did not over burden the house or property with servants. She had the housekeeper, who also seemed to serve as her companion and even the cook. There was one maid and a footman/errand boy, who was now currently carrying the heavy tray.

Without waiting for Austen's reply, Kate directed the servant to set down the tray. "Thank you, Jeremy. Right here on this side table should do nicely."

"Very good, Miss." The servant bowed and left the room.

"Are you having trouble with your correspondence?" Her tone was kind but curious.

"Not at all, I am finished."

"Finished? Already?" A look flit across her face that was a combination of consternation and irritation. "Men are the worst possible correspondents," she declared with a laugh.

"No doubt you are right, but it shall serve the purpose of allaying any concerns my daughter might be having for my safety and telling her that I shall re-join her soon. I don't really see a need to go into any further detail."

All she did was laugh, which Austen couldn't decide if it were highly irritating or amusing. So he chose to ignore it. "Could I trouble you for some sealing wax?"

"Of course, no trouble at all," she responded instantly, hurrying over to her desk to get it.

Once he had his letter straightened out, he was swept with the uncomfortable feeling that he ought to express his appreciation for all that Kate was doing for him, but he couldn't come up with the right words. How do you thank someone for turning your life around?

"Why are you doing this?" he asked, overwhelmed with his feelings all of a sudden.

"Doing what?" She seemed genuinely confused by his question.

"Being so generous and kind to a stranger," he explained patiently. "You could have left me on the side of the road where you found me, or had a magistrate see to me, or even if you had thought you ought to see to my immediate needs, you could have sent me on my way the first morning. This, helping me learn how to get my life straightened out, is above and beyond the usual efforts of human kindness."

Kate blushed rosily at his words, much to Austen's fascination. It was a strange reaction. As though she had something to hide. Curious, he tilted his head, trying to see into her mind. Which was impossible with anyone, especially a beautiful woman. He grinned.

She busied herself pouring the tea and arranging everything precisely, avoiding eye contact.

"Do I make you nervous, Kate?" he asked, incredulous.

She nodded.

"Why?" He knew his bald question was a trifle rude given her obvious discomfort, but he could not fathom why the girl would be nervous in his presence.

Her blush deepened, but she finally looked at him, squarely in the eyes. "I haven't been much in a gentleman's company since my husband was killed, and you are a handsome man. It makes me nervous."

Austen's grin stretched across his face. "You think I'm handsome?" He found her words hard to believe but was warmed by the possibilities.

He began to worry for her health, as her face grew even darker. The poor girl looked beside herself with discomfort. But she gave him honesty. "Of course. You are handsome, my lord. And seeing you trying to better your situation is strangely attractive as well."

He felt like he was gaping over her words. "That is a rather cruel thing to jest about Mrs. Appleton."

Now she was gaping at him. "I would not jest about such a thing," she insisted. "And do not use that tone with me. Just because you are an attractive man does not give you leave to speak to me as though I were a simpleton."

"Thinking me attractive makes you a simpleton," he muttered as he shuffled his feet.

They looked at one another, both highly uncomfortable. Austen finally broke the awkward silence. "Well, I think you're beautiful, so I should be grateful that you think me attractive."

Her colour had finally been returning to a more natural hue, but his words brought the blush back to her cheeks. She could not bring her gaze to his face, instead focusing on his shoulder as she backed toward the door. "I think I hear Mrs. Peabody calling for me. I should go."

Austen couldn't hear anyone else's voice, but he did not prevent her departure. He had a lot he needed to think about, and some time alone would be most beneficial.

He stayed in the library until he was called for supper. Austen made every effort to be personable and nonconfrontational during the meal. It was interesting to note that Mrs. Peabody kept shooting quizzical glances between him and Kate throughout the evening. He excused himself early as it had been a long day.

Chapter Ten

Back in London

The morning after the Roxborough ball, Anne lay abed later than usual. It had been a late night and she'd had a bit of difficulty falling asleep as well. There were so many things to think about! She was still anxious about her father. And while she was beginning to enjoy her Season, thanks to the viscount and his friends' interference, she had some decisions to make about her future. It would be lovely if she had a parent with whom to discuss it all.

"Good morning, my lady," Sally sang out cheerily as she threw open the curtains. "I was surprised that you had not yet rung for me. Are you feeling poorly this morning?"

"Not in the sense of being ill, no, thank you for asking, Sally."

"In what sense then?" The kindly maid was observant enough to notice Anne's half-hearted answer.

"I had trouble getting to sleep last night, so I slept later than usual and am feeling a little worn around the edges this morning. Nothing to be too worried about."

"Oh, dear, milady, should I shut the drapes and let you go back to sleep?" Sally was contrite.

"No, no, Sally, it is high time for me to be up and about. There could be callers in a couple of hours, and I need to be fed and dressed properly if anyone does stop by."

Sally handed Anne her cup of chocolate and asked with a coy tone, "Is there anyone in particular you are hoping calls by?"

Anne's sigh was both disconsolate and frustrated. "Does it sound foolish to say I cannot answer that question?"

Sally frowned at her mistress. "Not foolish, no, but you certainly sound like you need to talk the matter through. I don't know any of the *ton's* gentlemen, as it has been ages since her ladyship entertained before you came, but if you're just needing a listening ear, I'd be happy to help."

"Thank you, Sally." Anne sipped her chocolate and pondered her problem. "For one thing, I am becoming quite anxious about my father. While he has been less than reliable over the years, especially since my mother passed away, I know he cares about me and would not go off for long without telling me. Despite my aunt telling me that her husband suggested my father should leave, I really don't think he would have just gone off without at least saying goodbye." She paused again while the maid offered sympathetic noises but had no comment to offer.

Anne continued. "The Viscount of Bracondale has been most kind. He has set someone to searching for my father and has proven to be a real friend, much to my surprise. But he assures me he has no interest in gaining a wife at this point in life and, of course, I have no interest in him as a husband," she insisted. "I am not one of those silly girls who thinks she can reform a rake into an ideal husband." Anne ignored the flutter in her chest over this thought.

"No, I can see why you would say so, milady."

"Last night I met a lovely gentleman, a baron from a village only a couple of hours away from my home. He seemed quite pleasant and even wanted to introduce me to his mother."

"That sounds encouraging, milady."

Anne smiled at the maid. "It does sound encouraging, doesn't it? I should be far more excited about it than I am." She sighed again. "Part of me just wants to go home to

Rowanwood and forget all about this idea of making an advantageous match. That is a large part of the reason why I wish my father was here, Sally. I wish I could discuss with him if this really is our only option. I do not want to let him down. But it feels like a terrible responsibility. How can I make a choice that will affect the rest of my life?" She could hear that her voice was becoming a little shrill by the end of her speech and tried to offset the effect by offering another smile to her listening maid.

"Well, now, milady, that is a lot to handle. But there's nothing saying that you have to make your mind up today or even tomorrow, is there?"

"No, but there have already been some betrothals announced. It makes me feel like I will miss my chance if I do not make haste."

The maid hmmed and looked pensive. "I can see that would be trying, but I think you're making this harder for yourself than it needs to be. You still have several weeks before this Season is over. Maybe you'll find this baron is perfect for you, or else you will find someone else who is even more so. Or your viscount will decide that he cannot live without you." The maid chuckled when she saw Anne's cheeks heat over her last words.

"That is not going to happen, Sally. But you are quite correct. I really ought not to make this more difficult for myself by thinking about the betrothals. I am already feeling pressured. Thinking about that just makes it worse."

Sally was right, Anne thought, while she couldn't help her figure out which gentleman would make a good husband, just talking out her worries helped them seem a little less overwhelming. She really wished there were a lady she could discuss these matters with, someone who would know who she was talking about.

No use crying over spilt milk, though, as her mother used to say. Thinking of her mother brought a sheen of tears to her eyes, but she willed them away. Another thing that could not be changed.

Anne threw back the covers, determined to get the day started and not allow her troubles to turn her into a melancholy mess.

"Never mind about my troubles, Sally, what I really need is a good meal. Do you know if the breakfast room is still spread or should we ring for a tray from the kitchen?"

"I don't think your aunt has been down to eat yet either, so everything should still be spread in the breakfast room, milady. It might not be very warm by the time you get there, though."

Anne wrinkled her nose. "Could you help me into a morning gown so that I could hurry down to eat? Then I will change into something more suitable for callers after I have been fed."

"Very well, milady."

She had the room to herself; even the footman who usually presided over the breakfast was elsewhere. Anne could not get quite comfortable in her aunt's house even if it was becoming more familiar. She longed for home as she ate her breakfast in silence. She made short work of it and was soon heading back upstairs to ready herself for the day.

The maid was surprised to see her. "Did you eat, milady? That was very fast."

"The room was empty and quiet, so I was not delayed by anything. Do not worry. I ate plenty." Anne didn't want the servant to be fussing over her, so she quickly changed the subject. "What should I wear today?"

Sally grinned. "You said you are expecting callers, is that right, milady?"

"Yes. I do expect that some will be by." Anne found herself flustered by the situation and sighed.

"I think the green sprigged muslin with the capped sleeves would be just the thing, milady." The maid didn't seem to notice Anne's discomfiture and followed through on her words, throwing wide open the wardrobe and extracting the mentioned gown.

"Oh, yes, that is a lovely choice." Anne thought her reply was weak, but since the servant didn't seem to notice, she didn't bother trying to cover it up. With another small sigh, she stripped out of her morning gown and allowed the maid to button her into the new one. Sally didn't seem to be in any hurry, taking her time with Anne's hair. It actually was a relaxing experience, having her hair done, and Anne allowed her mind to drift as the maid brushed and pinned her locks into place. Absently, Anne reflected that she was relieved that even though her hair was a nondescript, mousy sort of brown, she was glad to see that it was shiny, healthy looking, and held the style the maid twisted it into without too much difficulty.

Sally was just sliding in the last pin when Anne was jolted out of her reverie by the sound of the knocker on the front door. She searched her reflection critically but saw that everything was in place.

"Thank you, Sally. It looks like we may have finished just in time."

She stood from the dressing table and headed for the door just as there was a tap on her bedroom door. Sally hurried to answer it. A footman was waiting with the message that Anne had callers waiting. Exchanging a smile with the maid, Anne followed the footman out of the room.

There was a steady bustle of activity as callers came and went. Anne's newfound popularity certainly enlivened the day. It was a shame that she didn't enjoy gossip as much as her callers seemed to, but she still managed to enjoy the visitors.

The Viscount of Bracondale had arrived just moments before and was busy exchanging pleasantries with a couple of ladies on the other side of the room when the baron was shown into the room with his mother in tow. Anne saw Lord Dunbar's eyebrows rise sardonically just as she turned to welcome her newest arrivals.

"Lady Halstead! How lovely to see you this morning," Anne greeted as she dipped into a curtsy. Please, have a seat here on the settee. Are you acquainted with everyone else here?"

"Of course, my dear." Her reply was proud but not unkind. The baroness sat where Anne had indicated and gazed around the room. Her eyes lit up when Anne's aunt bustled into the room.

"Lady Halstead," Lady Sophie greeted. "What a charming surprise to find you here."

"I had no idea you were sponsoring a niece for the Season, my dear," Lady Halstead explained. "When my son mentioned a desire to call by, I was delighted by the thought of catching up with my dear old friend."

Anne was pleasantly surprised to see how happy her aunt seemed to be about the callers. She sat down and launched into a cosy visit with her old friend, leaving Anne to entertain the baron.

"I was hoping you could get to know my mother a little bit," the baron explained as he looked around the room. "I didn't realize you would have so many visitors this morning, nor that she would be so taken with your aunt." He seemed chagrined, so Anne hastened to reassure him.

"That is fine, my lord, do not trouble yourself that I am put out by it. I am happy to see Lady Sophie's delight in seeing her old friend. It is often strange to think of our elders as once being young girls making their own debut, is it not? It is a good reminder seeing the two of them together like that."

"You are quite correct, my lady, and so gracious to take it in your stride."

Anne blushed and demurred. "It would be ridiculously churlish to do otherwise, would it not, my lord?"

The baron looked unconvinced, so Anne went on to add, "I think you might be in need of new friends if any one of your acquaintances were to begrudge your mother spending time with an old friend."

She decided it was time to turn the subject. With a soft giggle, she asked, her tone teasing, "Has your mother set her sights on any potential new stepfathers for you yet?"

His pained but amused expression rewarded her efforts. She was happy to see that he had a sense of humour. "She said she is still observing, determining who is available, before she makes her intentions known to any particular gentleman."

Anne managed not to giggle again but found that she was highly curious. "How long was she married to her previous husband?"

"Almost six years. My father died just over seven years ago. The day her mourning for my father ended, she came to me and said she couldn't stand being a widow and she was going to find herself another husband. I must say, it was rather a shock at first. We tend to consider our parents to be fixtures, and it is difficult to see them as separate entities who wish to marry someone other than your other parent. Even though he was dead, at first it felt disloyal. But her second husband was a decent man who made her happy for six years. I do not begrudge her that happiness. So, I will do what I can to help her find another husband if that is what she wishes."

"I'm sorry you lost your father so young, my lord."

He looked at her surprised. "You must have been much younger than me when you lost your mother."

She laughed lightly. "Thus my sympathy, my lord, I know exactly how difficult it is."

The baron sighed and passed his hand through his hair, leaving some strands standing in a manner that she found endearing, revealing a degree of frustration the usually even-tempered nobleman was not wont to show.

Feeling a rush of sympathy, Anne reached out and touched his arm gently. "It has to be a little strange to watch your mother courting. I know I would struggle a little with it if my father ever decided to remarry."

The baron put his hand over hers where it lay on his arm, a look of appreciation warming his eyes. They exchanged a smile.

Anne's faltered momentarily as she glanced across the room and saw the viscount watching them with a glower upon his face. Quickly averting her eyes from his intense gaze, she brightened her smile at the baron but pulled her hand back from his grasp.

The clatter of new arrivals ended the moment between Anne and Lord Seymour as she went over to welcome Lord Grey and the Earl of Sutton.

"My lady," they both greeted her and kissed her hand gallantly, bringing a genuine smile to her face.

"The two of you could charm the birds out of the trees. It amazes me that you have not yet been hunted down by all the match-making mamas of the *ton* as you are surely immensely popular."

As if to support her words, the air was punctuated by the giggles of some of the debutantes in the room who had spotted the noblemen at the door.

"We have ensured that our charm has boundaries, my lady." The earl's assurance was suave.

"Well, do come in and make yourselves useful by entertaining some of my callers. I am quite certain the ladies have called to see you, not me."

"I find that hard to believe, my lady, but we shall do our level best." Lord Grey winked at her as he passed her on the way to greeting others in the room, stopping first to be welcomed by Lady Sophie.

The interruption caused the baron's mother to come to her feet.

"Seymour, my boy, it is time we should be on our way," she called to her son. "Sophie, it was a delight to see you. And your lovely niece seems to be a success. I am certain we shall be seeing more of the two of you. We shall wish you a good day."

Anne wasn't sure how to respond to the woman's words, so she smiled and curtsied as they took their leave.

~~~
~~~

"One would almost think you had feelings for the lady, the way you are glowering at her suitors," the earl drawled to Wesley.

Wesley made every attempt to brazen it out. "Is that not the point of our presence? To give the impression that we are taken with her? So that others will follow suit and she can garner some offers of marriage."

"We did that, it worked, now she has suitors. Unless you wish to cultivate expectations in the poor woman's mind, you ought to pull back a little, Dunbar. Even I am wondering if you might have actual feelings for her."

"Do not be absurd, Sutton, have I ever given you reason to think I have any desire to become leg shackled?"

"Not up until now," came the swift reply.

"Well, I have not all of a sudden changed my thoughts on the subject. I just cannot feel quite settled that the baron is a good match for her."

"Why ever not?" Sebastian demanded. "He's well to do, reasonably intelligent, and reputed to be a kind, gentle soul. It's actually rather perfect in my estimation. Besides the fact that it would appear that he has a genuine interest in the lady, unlike us."

"But his mother! Do you really think Lady Anne ought to be saddled with her as a mother-in-law?"

His two friends looked at him as though he had lost his mind. Wesley wondered for a moment if they might be right, but then he shoved the idea impatiently from his mind. He stared at his friends belligerently. Their incredulous looks were tinged with pity, but then they shrugged and laughed.

Soon, Anne's callers had all trickled out and her aunt was seeing out the last couple of the ladies. Wesley was glad to see that he and his friends would have her to themselves for a moment.

"Did you receive my invitation for an evening at the theatre?" he demanded without preamble.

He was gratified to see her look of delight. "We did, yes, thank you, my lord. Did my aunt not send you an acceptance? I am quite looking forward to it."

Wesley nodded. "I haven't read my correspondence yet today, but I am glad the date is acceptable to you."

"You are going to an awful lot of trouble for me, my lord. Surely it is no longer necessary, as I seem to have garnered sufficient interest."

"We need to see this thing through to completion," he insisted before concluding, "Besides, I gave you my word, and I intend to keep it."

She clasped her hands in front of her, looking enchantingly earnest. "Well, I do appreciate it, Lord Dunbar, and I look forward to the evening at the theatre." She turned to the other gentlemen. "Will you be attending as well?"

They looked at Wesley, mocking grins on their faces. "We did not yet receive our invitations."

Wesley watched closely as Anne blushed and looked away. He wondered what was going on inside her head. Was she embarrassed by her question or gratified by his friends' reply? He dismissed his thoughts. There was a reason he was spending time with the chit, and it did not involve having feelings for her, he reminded himself.

"You seemed to be pretty cosy with Lord Seymour," he commented, watching the surprise on her face.

"There was nothing inappropriate about our association," she protested.

"I didn't say there was." His reply was verging on snide. He noticed his friends looking at him dubiously.

"It was kind of the three of you to stop by," Anne said, clearly dismissing them, much to Wesley's amusement. The chit was a delight, he thought with a grin. He watched as she did her best to stand firmly gracious, despite her nerves.

The earl was the first to graciously accept being dismissed. "We shall see you this evening, my lady. Save me a dance," he added with a wink.

Sebastian didn't bother saying anything, just bowed over her hand and took his leave. Wesley was the last to go. He recognized the discomfort in her eyes and decided not to make her any more uncomfortable than she already was. He bowed, making her an elegant leg and kissed her wrist.

He held onto her wrist, knowing he was probably invading her space, but he didn't want his friends to hear what he said. "You looked lovely this afternoon, my dear. And you handled your callers like an experienced matron. You are a success and should be proud of yourself."

He had no intention of upsetting her, so he was shocked when her eyes welled with tears and her lip trembled. Thunderstruck, he was swept with the urge to pull her into his arms and comfort her. He resisted the impulse but did tighten his grip on the hand he was still holding.

"My apologies, my lady, I did not wish to upset you."

Tears still swam in her eyes as she smiled tremulously at him. "You did not upset me, my lord. It is just that that was the nicest compliment anyone has ever given me, and it touched my heart. Thank you for saying such a reassuring thing."

The look on her face made Wesley think she was wishing she could do something more than just squeeze his hand, as though she wanted to throw her arms around him. While he would no doubt enjoy that, it certainly would not do, so he took a step back from her and finally released her hand.

He bowed again, and with a teasing note to his voice he told her, "I, too, shall see you tonight. Don't save just any old dance for me, my dear, I expect you to save me a waltz."

This must have been just the right note, as she took it for a joke and offered him a watery sounding chuckle. "Good day, my lord, and thank you for coming."

Wesley strode from the room, restraining himself from looking back to see if she were watching him. He could feel her gaze but resisted the urge to wave. He would see her again within a few hours.

~~~

His friends were waiting for him on the front steps of Lady Sophie's house. "What took you so long?" grumbled Sebastian. "Have you no idea how thirsty that has made me?"

Wesley chuckled. "Come along then. The club shall quickly make short work of your thirst."

"But seriously, Dunbar, what did take you so long?" the earl asked quietly. "You weren't giving Lady Anne any trouble, were you? She has been handling the attention we have garnered for her quite graciously, and I think we should be advising her, not admonishing her. In fact, she might not even require our advice. I know we started this venture with serious misgivings about the chit, but I think she is a nice young lady who was sadly misguided before we came along. You need to offer her your support, not the rough edge of your tongue."

Wesley was surprised but gratified by his friend's words. "You are absolutely correct, Sutton. And no, I was not ringing a peal over her. I was just taking a moment to say a few words to her as I did not get to talk to her, despite being there for much longer than was perfectly acceptable. It seems as though we have done our job too well, and she is too popular. Some of her callers cannot even get to exchange words with her!"

"I hardly think anyone is feeling slighted when they visit her," the earl pointed out reasonably. "From what I could see, she was a gracious hostess and all her guests were enjoying themselves."

The viscount could not explain what he had meant, so with impatience he blurted, "Never mind about that, let us head to the club and assuage Sebastian's thirst. I could certainly join him in tossing back a glass or two."

The other two men exchanged amused glances but did not argue with their friend. Before long, they were ensconced in their usual seats being served their favourite brandy.

After a couple of glasses, Wesley turned to his friends, no longer able to keep his concerns to himself.

"I think I've found her father," he said without preamble.
~~~

"Whose father?" Sebastian was puzzled.

"Lady Anne," Wesley answered, keeping his voice low and glancing around to ensure they were not being overheard.

The earl laughed. "I think you are turning into a fribble, Dunbar, it would appear you can no longer hold your liquor."

Wesley scowled at his friend. "I can hold my brandy just fine, but that doesn't mean I know what to tell her ladyship about her father."

His two friends eyed him for a moment, waiting to see if he would elaborate. "I did not realize Lord Austen was missing," the earl stated carefully.

Wesley shrugged. "There has not been a hue and cry about it, but her ladyship is concerned about his whereabouts."

"And this prompted you to mount a search?" the earl prompted, his eyebrows elevated.

"Don't look at me like that, Sutton. We agreed the chit is our responsibility. She was worried, so I said I would look into it. Nothing in it to make you look like that."

"If you say so," Sutton replied with an amused grin.

"So, what did you find out?" Sebastian demanded.

"Not sure if I should tell you two before discussing it with her ladyship."

"Then why did you even bring it up?" Sebastian seemed disgusted.

"All right, children, don't get yourselves tied in a bunch," Sutton soothed, restraining his laughter. "Finish your drinks. It's high time we got on our way. If we are to meet up with our lady, we ought to hie ourselves home and change our togs."

Chapter Eleven

Anne was dressed and ready, every hair tucked precisely into place, her new kid slippers comfortable on her feet. She waited until she heard her aunt and uncle making their way down to the foyer. She did not want to face the teasing she would have to endure if she were downstairs before them.

"Very well, milady, I think you are set." The maid was looking at her quizzically, wondering why she had not yet left the room.

"Thank you, Sally." Anne did not bother to explain herself, knowing it would sound ridiculous if she even tried.

As soon as she reached the bottom of the stairs, Anne greeted her aunt. "You look lovely this evening."

"Oh, why thank you, my dear. You are in your looks this evening as well. I do believe the Season is agreeing with you."

Anne had no ready response to her aunt's words but was saved from having to do so by her uncle's impatience. "Come along, ladies, let us not keep the horses standing."

Anne couldn't help giggling over this. Was it not the horses' job to wait for them? She managed not to utter her rhetorical question. No doubt her uncle would not take well to her wit.

Despite leaving the house earlier than usual, there was still a long line of carriages waiting to disgorge their occupants at their destination. Anne recognized her uncle's irritation with the wait as he tapped his foot and fidgeted in the seat next to her aunt. Lady Sophie reached her hand out and touched her husband's knee.

"It won't be too many more minutes, my lord. Do try to contain yourself."

He made a sound of disgust in his throat. "This is all a bunch of foolishness, my lady. Why are we bothering with this Season business?"

Lady Sophie shot her husband a quelling look while Anne tried to swallow her guilt for her uncle's discomfort. "You needn't have accompanied us, my lord," she pointed out, obviously endeavouring to be reasonable.

"Well now, I couldn't let the two of you go traipsing about the city by yourselves at night without any sort of escort, now could I?" He looked at his wife with contrition shining in his face. "I should never have sent away the girl's father. For all he's a loose fish, he would have been a sufficient escort to allow you to gad about without me."

Anne wasn't sure if she should put her nose into the conversation, and she was certain she could not comment on her uncle's opinion of her father, but her guilt for involving her uncle rose to the fore. "Perhaps we could call upon the services of some of the gentlemen who call on me to offer their escort for the evening if you feel that it is such a trial for you, Uncle. Then you need not worry about us, and we need not inconvenience you."

Her uncle smiled kindly at her. "You are a good girl for thinking of that, but I'm not so sure I should allow the two of you to go off with just anyone."

"No, of course not just anyone, my lord. But perhaps we shall be able to think of a solution." Anne averted her face by gazing out the window into the darkness beyond their carriage. She was swept with a desire to be home at Rowanwood once more.

"The girl has a good idea, my lord." Aunt Sophie stepped into the silence. "It will be far more enjoyable for her and me if we don't have to worry about you glowering at us. If she has callers tomorrow, I will see if any of them would be suitable as an escort." She turned to Anne. "Perhaps that lovely Lord Seymour would be willing. I am certain his mother would be glad for our company."

Anne smiled at her aunt but held her silence.

Finally, their carriage lurched forward. They were at the front of the line, and it was their turn to disembark. As Anne climbed the stairs, holding her skirts away from her feet, she looked up at the elegant home they were about to enter. Every window glowed with the light from within, and she could see that the rooms were already becoming crowded. Since they were so early, guests would continue to arrive for at least another hour. She felt a slight shudder at the thought of the crowds. Memories of home made her almost weep with longing. She shoved the thoughts from her head and concentrated on the evening before her. She needed to determine her future so evenings like this could be an occasional experience rather than a nightly one.

More heads turned as she and her aunt were announced, and she was grateful for the beautiful gown her aunt had gifted her. She fingered the fabric to give her hands something to do as she fought to control her nerves at the attention she was garnering. Young ladies and gentlemen came near to greet her, and her nerves ratcheted up another notch. Taking a deep breath, she prayed she could remember everyone's names as she returned greetings and made conversation.

Anne saw out of the corner of her eye her aunt's satisfied smile as she watched Anne fielding the attention of so many. Anne was glad her aunt was happy with her success. She was surprisingly ambivalent about it herself. She was grateful for the help of Lord Dunbar and his friends, but this much attention was a little difficult for her to manage. For the thousandth time, she wished her mother were there. She shoved that thought from her mind as well. It would not do to begin weeping in the middle of the crowded ballroom.

That thought brought a smile to her face, and she was able to carry on. When the orchestra started to play, it became easier. As she passed from gentleman to gentleman, the evening began to pass in a blur. And then Lord Dunbar came to claim his waltz.

"You have been busy this evening," he commented with a smile that did not quite reach his eyes.

"Yes," Anne replied without elaborating, wondering why he seemed displeased.

"Are you enjoying yourself?" he asked, his kind tone causing her to search his face for answers she could not find.

"Somewhat, my lord. I do not wish to disparage Lady Talbot's hospitality, but I cannot say I enjoy the crowds at events such as these. Actually, everywhere I have been since I arrived in London is crowded. Except for that drive you took me on to Uxbridge. That was a breath of fresh air."

"Many of the debutantes love the crowds."

Anne sighed. "Yet another proof that I am not like other girls." Her disconsolate tone caused the viscount to chuckle quietly. The sound caused a not unpleasant flutter in Anne's chest.

"I do not hate the crowds as much as you seem to, but I cannot blame you for not enjoying these events."

"Why do you keep coming if you don't like them, my lord? You have said quite plainly that you have no wish to get married, so it seems rather contradictory to be at all the *ton* events."

"I have a friend here that needs watching," the viscount said with a teasing tone.

Anne felt heat creeping into her cheeks. "You needn't continue, my lord. I think you have done enough to ensure my success. I strongly doubt I would do the same for you."

Again, the viscount chuckled over her words. "Well, that is certainly putting me in my place, my dear. But never mind, it isn't such a trial, there is much to amuse me at balls and routs.

And, of course, there is our evening at the theatre to look forward to."

"Oh, yes, I do hope I can keep my hopes under control. I would hate to be disappointed because I have allowed my expectations to get out of hand." Anne couldn't help grinning with her anticipation.

The viscount turned the subject abruptly. "Have you settled on any one of your suitors yet? Does it seem that any particular gentleman is likely to come up to scratch?"

Anne felt it was somehow inappropriate to be discussing such things with the viscount, but she ignored the thought as there was no one else she could talk to about it. "No one has made an actual offer yet, no, but a couple of gentlemen have become quite marked in their attentions. I have been receiving deliveries of flowers most days, which is quite delightful." She offered him a dimpled grin but followed it up with a sigh. "The only trouble is that I feel like I want to discuss these gentlemen with my father, but he has still not returned, nor have I received any word from him." She looked up eagerly at the viscount. "Do you have any more information about him?"

"As a matter of fact, I have found further trace of him."

"Well, why didn't you say so earlier?" She almost stamped her foot with frustration at the nonsensical lord.

"We were speaking of other things," he replied, but she could see that he was fighting to control his smile.

She rolled her eyes. "Well, what have you found out?" she demanded.

"I believe he was set upon by footpads and sustained some injury but has been taken in by a kindly widow in the village of Beaconsfield. From what the Runner could find out, his injuries were not overly serious, but that is no doubt what is preventing his return."

"Were his fingers broken?" she asked, sounding peeved, which again made the viscount smile. "Did his injuries somehow prevent his sending me a message?"

"It is possible that he had a head injury and has lost his memory," the viscount offered with another chuckle before continuing in an obvious effort to offer comfort. "My lady, you must realize that men often do not consider that anyone might be worried about them. I know when I was away at school my mother would always lament that I so rarely wrote to her."

"But you were a boy, my lord, not someone's father."

"True, but I'm sure you would agree that there is often very little difference between boys and men."

This funny statement finally broke through Anne's anger, and she couldn't help but laugh. "You are right, my lord, I need to try to keep my mind open. And I should be relieved that he is not dead or on a ship to the colonies. So you have this widow's direction so I could write to him, or her maybe, if he has in fact lost his memory."

"I shall get it to you tomorrow. In the meantime, while he is still absent, would you care to discuss your marital options with me?"

"With you? How could we do that, my lord? I would be absolutely mortified if we were to be overheard." Anne was gratified by his offer but doubted it could be practically carried out.

"I could call round for you one afternoon after your callers have left and take you for another drive. If we go to the Park before it gets too crowded we should be able to be fairly private but perfectly respectable."

"That is a graciously kind offer, thank you, my lord. I have already accepted Lord Cumberland's invitation to go driving tomorrow, but the following day would be lovely."

"Very well, I shall call for you then."

Their arrangement was perfectly timed, just as their waltz came to an end and Lord Seymour stepped forward to claim her hand for the next dance.

The dances all swirled into one another and before she knew it, Anne was getting tucked up into her bed at her aunt's house, feeling sleepy and content.

When she arrived in the breakfast room the next morning, her uncle was just finishing up. "There is a letter for you, my dear. Whenever you're ready, ask the butler for it."

"A letter for me?" Anne was excited to hear that, hoping it was news from her father. She could not settle down to eat without finding out. She curtsied to her uncle and hurried from the room.

A few minutes later she returned to the breakfast room, disappointed by her father's sparse words but relieved to know he had remembered about her and that he was well. He had even provided a return address, so she determined to write back to him as soon as she had eaten.

Her uncle was half hidden behind his newspaper as he sipped his coffee, but he noticed her return and lowered the paper a little to ask solicitously, "I trust it was good news?"

"Yes, thank you, my lord, it was." She didn't elaborate, mindful of her uncle's words the night before that he had asked her father to leave.

The rest of the day passed in a blur. She had several callers, Lord Cumberland took her for an uneventful drive in the Park, and she attended a rout in the evening. The rout was less crowded than the balls she had attended, but not by much. She returned home nearly as exhausted as from a ball, sinking gratefully into her soft bed and drifting off into a dreamless sleep.

~~~

She tried to quell her eagerness to see Lord Dunbar, but despite her efforts to think of other things, the morning dragged uncomfortably. She was relieved when the knocker sounded, signalling the arrival of her afternoon's callers. That certainly sped the day along and with a smile, she waved away the last of her callers and hurried up to her room to change into a riding habit. It crossed her mind to wish they were actually going to be riding instead of driving, but that would not lend itself as well to conversation, and she was quite
~~~

looking forward to her upcoming inappropriate conversation with the viscount. It was so unexpected that he had become her friend, but she was grateful for it.

Just as the maid was pinning her hat at a jaunty angle over her elaborate coiffure, the knocker was heard sounding once more throughout the house. Glancing into the mirror, Anne saw that her high colour reflected her excitement. She sternly admonished herself to calm down. She ought not to be so excited about a ride with the unavailable viscount. Then she reminded herself that she was just looking forward to discussing her marital options. With that thought, she took a deep breath and opened the door just as the footman was about to knock, summoning her to meet her caller.

"Thank you, Jason, I am on my way," she said with a smile.

She wanted to hurry but did not want to appear too eager, so she forced her feet to a sedate pace. The viscount was waiting patiently in the foyer. She was gratified to see his delighted smile at her appearance.

"My lady," he began with a flourishing bow, "you are looking lovely, as usual, this afternoon."

She tried not to simper as she accepted the compliment. She was quite sure it would give him a disgust of her. She couldn't quite fathom why she was so delighted to see him. He could be decidedly disagreeable at times, and there was that threat of ruining her that should have been completely off putting. But she couldn't seem to help it; she was happy to see the contrary man.

Keeping herself still to a sedate walk and not the skipping she longed to do, she accompanied the viscount to his waiting phaeton. It was a sporting vehicle, not the carriage he had brought last time, and somehow that added one more notch to her excitement.

~~~

Wesley watched her eyes sparkling. While she was not usually moping, she was a serious sort of female, and he was
~~~

glad to see a little more *joie de vie* shining from her today. He felt inexplicably proud at the thought that it might be his presence that was making the young lady so cheerful. When her eyes landed on his phaeton, they lit up even brighter and he couldn't help chuckling. "You do not strike me as a thrill seeker, but I can see that you like the look of my conveyance."

She clapped her hands like a school girl, and he was surprised that it was not off putting. "Oh my lord, shall we be putting your horses through their paces today?" she asked, thankfully without a giggle.

"If you would like, that could certainly be arranged. Although driving at break-neck speed will not be conducive to conversation."

Her face fell at his reminder. But then she perked up. "Why do we not circle through the Park and then come out on the far end and take the road around the Park? There we should be able to see what your cattle have in them."

Wesley couldn't help chuckling over her words. It was a sound suggestion. "Very well, my lady, your wish shall be my command," he said, listening to her tinkling laughter as he handed her up into the high perched vehicle.

They made their way carefully through the crowded streets and entered the Park to see that it was already getting busy but was not yet crowded.

"Did you have many callers this afternoon?" he asked, making polite conversation as he kept his eyes on the road.

"I did, my lord. I was actually worried they would not get out in time for me to get ready before you arrived. But once Miss Fanshaw stood up to leave, most followed her lead." Anne paused and cast him a glance from beneath her eyelashes. "Did you make some sort of arrangement with her, too, my lord? She's prodigiously popular."

"She's a Diamond of the first water, my dear. She would not require anyone's help."

"No, of course not." Her small voice and brief reply made him look sharply at her. He realized with a shake of his head that he had not answered her question with an ounce of tact.

"There was no implication about you in my words, my dear."

"Perhaps not, my lord, but I did need help," she replied, but then hurried to try to save face. "Do not trouble yourself about my feelings, my lord. I am quite well aware that I am no Diamond. And I am decidedly grateful for your help. Even Miss Fanshaw visits me."

Her brave smile made Wesley long to tuck her under his arm and protect her from all hurts. He thrust the ridiculous notion from his mind and turned to more prudent thoughts.

"So, tell me, Lady Anne, have any of your gentleman callers become more overt in their attentions?"

She wrinkled her nose in a manner that was becoming familiar and endearing. "I do not know about overt, but several gentlemen have been sending me flowers and notes. A couple are calling round nearly every day. And Lord Seymour brought his mother with him."

"How do you feel about that?"

"About all of it? Or about Lord Seymour's mother?"

Wesley laughed. "Both."

Anne sighed. "It is actually a trifle stressful, to be honest. I thought I wanted to have choices, but what if more than one gentleman makes me an offer?" She turned to him with a horrified look on her face. "To have to tell others no when I have been allowing them to call and send gifts will be awkward to say the least."

"I do not think you need to worry too much about it, my dear. This is how these things go. The gentlemen are not blind. Surely they have noticed the other callers and even the numerous bouquets and posies about the house when they visit."

Again, she wrinkled her nose and then her smile widened. "That is an excellent point, my lord. I am so relieved to be having this discussion with you despite how unconventional it might be."

"Is there anyone in particular you hope does come up to scratch?" Wesley couldn't say why he held his breath while he waited for her reply.

"I wish I was a little more enthusiastic about it," she answered him on another soft sigh. "Lord Seymour has been lovely. He seems to be kind, gracious, and generous. It is encouraging to see how he treats his mother. But I wonder if his mother might be a problem. She seems to be nice enough, but she does demand a great deal of his attention. Of course, she has determined that she wants another husband, so perhaps she wouldn't be too much of a problem."

Wesley grinned over her soliloquy. "You seem to be talking yourself in circles, my dear."

"I know," she answered glumly.

"Is there anyone else who might be a better option?"

Her shrug was half hearted. "There is the earl, Lord Westlake. He has been very kind. He is a lovely dancer. From what my aunt and uncle tell me, he is plump in the pocket and needs an heir. But while he has been calling, and has sent me flowers, and makes a point of speaking to me at every social occasion, I am not convinced his heart is in it. I really don't think he is quite ready to settle down and start his own family."

"What gives you that impression? It would be rather unsavoury of the man to be raising expectations if he has no interest in following through."

"You are right, my lord, and I do not wish to speak ill of him. He has been nothing but kind to me, but it just feels as though he lacks enthusiasm, or he's just going through the motions. It is almost as though someone has told him he must get married, but he is not convinced of the truth of it."

Wesley nodded; he couldn't help but agree with her assessment. "At least you don't seem too broken up about it."

"I am beginning to wonder if there is something wrong with me. Most of the other debutantes are in alt over one or more gentlemen and cannot cease jabbering about them, wondering when or if they will propose and giggling madly whenever their eyes meet. For me, while I find most of the gentlemen quite pleasant, very few of them generate in me the least desire to giggle."

Wesley saw that she was quite serious, but her statement made him want to laugh. He struggled to contain himself. He was rather disgusted with himself for feeling relieved that she had not yet given her heart to any of her suitors. It was churlish of him. It would be much better for her if she would.

"Well, let us think a little more about Lord Seymour then. Do you see any true impediment to a match with him?"

She shrugged briefly. "No, not really. It is merely my lukewarm feelings on the matter that are giving me pause. He really is a catch, and I should be gratified that he is considering me." She sighed softly and then turned to him with earnest eyes. "Could you talk some sense into me, Lord Dunbar?"

Wesley smiled. He really could not muster up any enthusiasm for the task, but he knew he ought to. "I know many of the ladies consider him to be quite handsome."

"That is true. His eyes are a lovely shade of hazel, and I do like his smile."

The viscount gritted his teeth and continued. "He has a fine reputation for how he treats his animals."

She looked at him, momentarily puzzled by his words but then a soft smile touched her lips. "I never thought of it, my lord, but you have a point. How a man treats his animals *is* probably an indication of how he would treat his wife, since they are both in his power." She glanced at his horses. "It would seem you would be a generous and loving husband if your own beautiful horses are anything to go by."

They both shared a nervous laugh over her words. She quickly sobered. "I ought to try to get a look at Lord Westlake's horses the next time he comes to call."

"If we're going to base our judgment on how a man treats his cattle, I would suggest you strike Westlake off your list, my dear. Last year, one of his horses had to be put down because he forced it over a jump it didn't want to take, and the poor beast broke its leg."

"Oh no!" Her soft sound of distress made Wesley reach over and pat her hand where it rested in her lap.

"Is there anyone else you are considering? I could tell you what I know about their animals."

Now she looked mischievous. "Well, Lord Grey and Lord Spencer have been calling quite regularly, and they have not been as clear with me as you have that they are not in the market for a wife."

Wesley chuckled. "I can vouch for them as excellent carers of their animals, but I can assure you they would be aghast if they thought they had raised hopes in you."

"No, I am merely jesting with you. I was merely trying to illustrate how lost I am in this game." After a brief pause she turned the subject. "Did I tell you that I heard from my father yesterday?"

"No, you did not. Did he tell you where he is, or how he is, at least?"

"He was not very forthcoming, but he assured me that all is well and that he hopes to return to London within a few days. The trouble is, he did not date his note so I cannot say for certain when those days might be up. But at least it is something. He thought of me and finally realized he ought to let me know how he is. And you were right, he is still in Beaconsfield. Or rather he was at the time of writing, and that is the address he gave for me to write back."

She offered him a sunny, dimpled smile with those words, causing Wesley to catch his breath and wonder how the little mouse had turned into a beauty. He suddenly felt as though he couldn't say a thing. She didn't seem to notice.

"Now, I think I am talked out on the subject of my potential *beaux,* and I can see that the far exit of the Park is not too far away. What do you say to a dash around the perimeter road?"

"I say, let us proceed and hold onto your dashing hat, my lady." Wesley laughed as he prompted his horses to pick up their pace.

His companion laughed with glee as the scenery sped by. Within a few minutes, they were back into traffic and Wesley had to rein in his bays, but it had been lovely while it lasted.

"Thank you, my lord, this has been such a relaxing afternoon," Lady Anne said as she placed a hand softly on his arm and gazed up into his face with an earnest expression. Wesley was surprised to note that he fully agreed with her.

"The pleasure was mine, my dear." He made short work of steering through the traffic and within minutes, they were pulled up in front of her Aunt Sophie's house.

"Are you all set for the theatre tomorrow evening?" he asked as he handed her down from the high vehicle.

"I am, my lord, thank you. I am looking forward to it with great anticipation." Her twinkling eyes and cheerful grin made his hand squeeze reflexively where it still held hers, causing her to look at him in question.

He ignored her unspoken question, merely offering her as neutral smile as he could muster. "I will probably see you this evening, but if not, I shall see you on the morrow."

"Thank you, Lord Dunbar, I shall be seeing you."

Wesley watched as she made her way up the stairs and was admitted by the butler. He shook his head at himself as he finally prompted his horses to proceed. He really had to get that chit out of his head.

Chapter Twelve

The ball was in full swing by the time they arrived. Aunt Sophie and Anne had been invited to a dinner party hosted by Lord Seymour's mother. It had been quite a lovely experience, and Anne was feeling far more optimistic about the possibility of Lord Seymour proposing. She would have preferred her father being there to help her with this important decision, but it was looking as though she were going to have to muddle through on her own.

Aunt Sophie was of little help in the matter. She felt it all came down to the gentleman's bank balance.

"Under normal circumstances it would be decidedly *déclassé* to talk about money, my dear, as I am certain you are well aware. But when it comes to arranging a marriage, it is really all that matters. Especially for you, in your circumstances, there is really nothing else to consider as long as the man is accepted in polite Society," she had said to her on their way to the baron's home. "Lord Westlake is a lovely gentleman, but his pockets are not nearly so plump as Lord Seymour's."

Anne blushed just remembering the conversation. It had bordered on vulgar, in her opinion. While she was quite well aware that she and her father were living on a shoestring and might soon have to face their creditors, she did not think it was at all acceptable to actually talk about it, especially not in the predatory way that Aunt Sophie had done.

Of course, the old dear was right in a certain way. Anne couldn't be squeamish and hold out for a love match like some of the debutantes were wont to talk about. She was grateful that the gentleman who seemed most ready to come up to scratch was well off and attractive to boot. And the fact that his home was near Rosedale was icing on the cake.

She was glad that Lord Seymour's mother had thought to invite her to her dinner party. From the looks of it, it had been more intended for her to entertain her own marital prospects than for her son's benefit. It had been wildly entertaining to watch and listen to the older gentlemen vying for her attentions. It was even more delightful because one of her concerns about Lord Seymour had been whether or not his mother would be a burden. With it so obvious that the lady would be well able to catch herself another husband, Anne felt confident she could cast aside that particular concern.

It was impossible to quell the happy smile she knew was stretching her face, so she gave up trying. She was lost in thought and thus did not notice his approach, so she nearly jumped out of her skin when the viscount spoke to her.

"Good evening, my dear, you are looking well."

With her hand clutched over her heart, she turned to her wide gaze onto him. "My lord! You nearly startled a year off my life."

He laughed over her word choice. "I apologize, my lady. I didn't know you would not be expecting someone to speak to you in this crowd of people."

Anne's scalp itched from the heat of embarrassment that climbed into her face at his teasing. "I was wool gathering, my lord, and did not notice you. Please, forgive my inattention."

"There is nothing to forgive. But I was wondering if I could have a private word with you."

She raised her eyebrows in question at him. "Is that really necessary, my lord?"

"I have something I need to tell you, and it is not something I think you would want to hear in public view."

She searched his gaze, trying to read his thoughts, but all she saw was his kind, patient smile. Tucking her hand into his elbow, she returned his smile. "Very well, my lord, lead on."

The viscount led her out onto the terrace through a set of French doors that had been left open to allow for some air. It wasn't completely appropriate, but it would not ruin her to be found there. She did not demure.

"Are you having a good evening, my lord?" she asked, unsure why she wanted to put off hearing whatever he had to say.

"Not particularly," he grumbled. "There is a harpy here who has been pursuing me for more than one Season. It seems she is determined that now is the time for me to come up to scratch. Little does she know that I have absolutely no desire to be aligned with her. While the thought of getting leg shackled is repellent in theory, considering marriage to her is downright repugnant."

Anne couldn't help laughing over his words. "What is so very awful about her? And do I know her? Because your description puts me very much of a mind to make her acquaintance."

"Now you are just being vindictive," he said, mock outrage in his voice, causing another gurgle of laughter to bubble to her lips.

"Please, my lord, you must tell me. I shall perish from the curiosity if you do not."

"I cannot, as a gentleman, impugn her by telling you her name after I told you what I really thought of her."

Anne continued to grin. "Your ideas of gentlemanly conduct amuse me, my lord. If you were truly a gentleman, you would never have said the slanderous words in the first place."

"Now you're the one being a harpy," the viscount said but belied his words as he joined her in laughter.

"All right then, never mind about her. What did you have to tell me? Is it something about my father?"

Her nerves made her reach out and take hold of his hand without even realizing it. She was surprised when he patted her hand, obviously in an effort to offer her comfort. She made to pull back her hand, but he tightened his grip so she left it in his grasp, enjoying the thrill that shivered up her spine at the contact and almost forgetting the question she had asked.

"Yes, it is about your father."

"Is he all right? I just received his letter telling me not to worry two days ago. Has he been hurt worse than we thought?"

"Hush now, my lady, do not get yourself into a taking. His injuries were not any worse than we had been lead to believe. In fact, I suspect they were not serious at all. No, the matter is concerning the widow who has taken him in. It seems she is not the matronly type of widow we might have imagined. I am afraid she might be taking advantage of your father."

~~~

Wesley was enjoying holding Anne's hand far too much. He ought to let her go, he told himself, but he was concerned that she would be overcome by the news he had just shared. It was obvious to him that she did not comprehend what he was saying as she gazed at him, blinking rapidly. And then she burst into laughter.

"But my lord, there is nothing to take advantage of," she protested. "If she is after a man of means, she will catch cold at her efforts."

Wesley could see what she meant but tried to get her to see where he was coming from. "But my lady, how will you feel if your father was to remarry?"

"I would actually think it was lovely as long as I thought she was a woman who would treat him well. He deserves to be happy after all the sorrow we have faced, don't you think?"

Now it was Wesley's turn to blink at her. "Well, yes, of course, I do not wish to imply I wouldn't want your father to be happy, but would it not make you feel as though you were
~~~

losing your home?" He was starting to feel like a simpleton. He was actually trying to preserve her feelings, but it was starting to feel as though he was going to hurt them.

He saw her tilt her head as though she were studying him, and he wondered what she might see. "Would that not be rather churlish of me, my lord?" she asked. "I am here for the Season trying to find myself a new home. It would be rather awful if I wanted to horde my old one, too."

"Well, yes, of course," Wesley stammered as he felt heat stain his cheekbones, thankful for the low lighting out there on the terrace, hoping she would not notice.

"Of course, my easy-going attitude on the matter would be sure to change if I thought she was anything like your harpy, though. So, I do appreciate your concern. Do you think I ought to journey there and make sure they do not wed before I have had a chance to examine her?"

Wesley was delighted to see her all fired up on her father's behalf. He wondered what it would be like to have someone so caring about him. He shoved the random thought from his mind as he hurried to steady her.

"No, I do not think that is necessary. If you must know, the Runner actually had good reports about the woman, not at all someone you need be overly concerned about. I merely thought that you would be upset at the thought of someone taking your mother's place."

Anne shrugged, much to his surprise. "It would be impossible for anyone to take my mother's place. But I would be happy for my father to find happiness once again. I think our hearts are remarkably versatile. Loving someone else does not diminish the love you had for the one who is gone. The relationship my parents had was beautiful and special. But when my father lost my mother, he also lost part of himself, particularly the rational part of himself, which is what has brought us to where we are now in the first place. So, if she is a decent woman, I will be glad for it." She paused in thought for a moment, and Wesley found himself holding his breath once more. "But I do hope I get to meet her before she becomes my stepmother," she concluded with a grin.

"You, my dear, are delightful."

Anne laughed. "That's not what you were saying just days ago," she teased.

Wesley laughed with her. "Just as you said, the heart is versatile, I say, so is the mind. And I am not so mule headed that I cannot change my mind about something." He kept hold of her hand but then put it through his elbow once more. "Now come along, my dear, someone is sure to be missing you, so I ought to return you to the ballroom before a search party is mounted."

She tugged lightly on his arm just before they stepped through the open door. "Thank you for being my friend, my lord. I truly appreciate your concern."

"Think nothing of it, my lady. Is that not what friends do?"

He ignored the flutter in his chest at the sight of her delighted smile. They spotted Lord Grey as they stepped into the crowded room. Wesley handed her over to his friend, giving him a speaking glance.

Sebastian quickly bowed to Lady Anne and invited her onto the dance floor as Wesley promised to procure them glasses of punch.

~~~

That dance passed quickly, and when they left the dance floor, Lord Seymour was waiting to escort Anne into the cotillion. She was surprised the viscount had not returned with the promised punch, but she didn't bother much about it as they stepped into the familiar dance. She enjoyed the baron's company, what snippets of it she could as they separated and returned through the movements of the dance. Anne was amazed how quickly the evening was passing. Once again, a dance was coming to an end.

As Lord Seymour was escorting her from the dance floor, they noticed a commotion developing near them. The baron
~~~

tried to steer her away from an ill-bred scene, but Anne could hear Lord Dunbar's voice in the skirmish and ignored the baron's pressure on her arm. She wound her way through the gathering crowd with the baron on her heels.

Anne felt the blood draining from her head when she realized what was happening. *This must be Dunbar's harpy,* she thought faintly as she wondered desperately what she should do.

The young woman would be quite lovely if her features were not screwed up into a shrewish pout, Anne thought, almost dispassionately as she heard what the girl was saying to a man who could only be her father. "He took advantage of me, Papa, now you must do something about it."

The poor man looked as though he had been backed into a corner and had no acceptable way out. He looked suitably horrified, but it was unclear if it were directed at the viscount or his daughter as his gaze went back and forth between Dunbar and the harpy. "My dear, perhaps this is a conversation more suited to privacy," he began.

"No, this needs to be dealt with now. Privacy will not help."

Not help you trap Dunbar, you mean, Anne thought as she wrinkled her nose at the ill-bred scene playing out before her.

Lord Seymour had his hand on her elbow, obviously still eager to steer her away from witnessing whatever was to take place. "My lady, I do not think your aunt would wish you to be a party to this."

Anne ignored his suggestion. The viscount was her friend, and she could not leave him to this woman's mercies. Through the crowd, her eyes met his and she knew she would have to help if she could. Lord Dunbar looked angry and defiant and certainly not cowed by the woman's efforts. Perhaps he wouldn't need Anne's help after all, but she could not leave until she had verified for herself that he was all right.

Though he looked pained to do so, the harpy's father was asking her, "In what way has Lord Dunbar taken advantage of you?"

"He pulled me into our host's library and ravaged me."

Her father looked ready to faint. Dunbar looked ready to explode. The woman's mother arrived on the scene and added her shrill demands to the noise already being generated by the shocked glee of the milling spectators.

"He shall have to marry her," the mother declared, causing Anne to gasp. *Of course! But really*, she thought, her irritation making her caustic, *what parents in sound mind would want to tie their daughter for life to someone who held no respect for her person?*

"When did this take place?" the father thought to ask.

His daughter blinked, unprepared for an examination of her statement. "About fifteen minutes ago. It took me a few minutes to regain my composure in order to come and find you."

Anne couldn't keep silent. "So just before the country dance?"

The harpy turned to her with a glare. "I suppose so."

Anne's gaze once again met the viscount's. She saw that he suddenly realized what she was about to do, and he shook his head at her. Anne ignored him.

Her heart felt as though it were beating three times its usual pace, and her stomach wanted to empty its contents, but Anne could not stand by while Dunbar was vilified. She glanced back at the baron and was filled with regret for the lovely, safe life she was about to throw away. Wesley had been quite clear that he would not rescue her if she ruined herself over him, but she could not ignore his plight.

"He could not have been taking advantage of you because he was on the terrace with me at that time for at least fifteen or twenty minutes, and I am almost certain he had just arrived before we stepped out for our conversation."

While venturing out onto the terrace was only slightly questionable and not enough to ruin her, declaring it publicly like that would taint her sufficiently that she might have just consigned herself to a life of spinsterhood. She felt the baron recoil next to her as he dropped his hand from her elbow and stepped away from her side. She wanted to close her eyes and wake up in her room to find out this had been a bad dream, but she could not tear her eyes from the *tableau* in front of her.

The viscount looked as though she had knocked him in the head. While the harpy's declarations had obviously angered him, Anne's had made his face go pale and expressionless. Anne chewed on her lip with nerves as she watched the harpy's face go deep red and her eyes shot daggers at her. Anne wondered if the woman were going to attack her. She also wondered if anyone would intervene to protect her.

Suddenly, Lord Grey and Lord Spencer were on either side of her. They took her arms and almost dragged her away. To watching eyes, it would only look as though they were escorting her solicitously, but she was quite well aware that they would brook no argument. If she had dug in her heels, she had the impression they would have just picked her up and carried off. That thought almost made her smile.

"What were you thinking?" the earl demanded, his tone brimming with frustration despite the polite face he maintained.

"I couldn't stand there and allow that woman to do that to him." Anne tried to explain, but Lord Grey cut her off.

"Did you not think he could look after himself?" Unlike the earl, he was unable to keep the stormy expression off his face.

"Would it make you feel better to know I did not have a chance to actually think the matter through?" she muttered before asking, "Where are you taking me?"

"To your aunt," the earl answered, his tone grim. "And then we are going to dance."

"Dance?" Anne was slightly horrified. "But I thought we could go home now. Surely you do not expect me to stay here after that?"

"It is the only way to try to mitigate the damage you have done. If you can brazen it out, perhaps you will not be ruined."

"I should not be ruined because I did nothing wrong." Anne hated the hypocrisy of the *ton* in that moment and would not have minded if she would never again have to set foot in London.

"We shall see." Lord Spencer didn't bother to say anything more as they had arrived at the side of Lady Sophie. The older woman did not know the details, but she took in at a glance enough to realize what needed to be done.

"Oh Anne, what have you done?" she asked, disappointed. She didn't wait for a response. "Never mind. We'll deal with it later." She turned to Sebastian. "Stop looking so dramatic. You should laugh as though she made some witty remark."

Sebastian blinked at her aunt, looked at Anne, and actually obeyed Sophie's words. To Anne's ears it even sounded genuine. A bubble of hysteria sat in her throat, and she thought she might laugh too but worried she would not be able to stop if she began, so she managed to confine herself to an answering smile.

The orchestra had stopped in the face of the commotion, but they were hastily getting settled and striking up the next song. Anne was equally parts horrified and relieved when she heard it was a waltz and the earl was looking at her with clear intent. She didn't know if she could face the dance floor, but at least she would not have to endure multiple partners.

The earl didn't speak to her, keeping his face pleasant but impassive. Anne tried to explain. "There was no avoiding it. You really must understand. I promise you, I was not trying to entrap him in any way. Lord Dunbar was quite clear with me that he would not be making me an offer, no matter what I did. But I could not stand there and allow that harridan to slander him like that. The viscount is my friend, too, you know."

This time when he met her eyes, Anne saw compassion reflected in his steady gaze. "I know, my lady. Do not get into a taking over it. Perhaps it will blow over without much fuss."

As the dance continued, Anne thought with a sinking heart that there was little hope of that. The harpy could be heard wailing as she was escorted from the ball room, even over the sound of the music. Curious, speculative gazes were being cast toward Anne as she circled the room in the earl's arms.

"Are you sure I cannot go home now?"

"Quite sure. Grey will dance with you next. I don't think Dunbar should. If your aunt can find your uncle, he should lead you out, too. And then you can go home. Unless your baron returns to your side. Then there would be nothing to worry about." The earl paused for a moment. "But from the look that was on his face, I am not holding out too much hope for that."

"He must not have cared for me in the first place if he would so easily reject me," Anne replied, hoping her voice would not quaver to reveal the depth of her hurt.

"Then he is an idiot, my lady, and not worth your time."

There was a pause as Anne tried to process all that had happened. "Lord Dunbar did not look pleased," she commented.

"Did you expect he would be?" the earl inquired, his tone not unkind, almost curious.

"As I told you, I did not take the time to think over much before acting. But surely he must realize that I only meant to help him."

The earl's tone was neutral as he said, "Do not let it trouble you, my dear."

"But I essentially traded my happiness for his. I would expect him to at least try not to be angry with me."

Finally, the earl dropped his serious mien and chuckled, drawing a few eyes their way but not in a censorious way, much to Anne's relief.

As the earl had decreed, Anne danced with Lord Grey and then her uncle before he finally allowed that she could leave. She had not been given the cut direct by anyone, so she surmised that she had not been totally outcast. Anne found that she could not quite care. All she wanted to do was go home and pull the covers over her head and sleep for a week. And preferably, never see another member of the *ton* ever again. She was finally going to be able to do at least the first point in her wish list. She may not sleep for a week, but she was definitely going to leave orders not to be disturbed the next day.

Chapter Thirteen

"She said what? The chit actually expects that I ought to be grateful?"

They were in Lord Sutton's library; the hour was well advanced and the earl had dismissed his servants after a decanter had been brought for him and his two friends. Wesley was pacing in front of the blazing fire that was attempting to chase the chill from the room.

"She told me she traded her own happiness for yours, so she expects you not to be angry with her."

"That's rich!" the viscount replied with disgust. He tossed back a large swallow of the earl's fine brandy, enjoying the burn as it slid down his throat. "I could see her clearly as it was happening, but I was too far away to be able to stop her. I know full well she thought she was doing it for me, and it was not a ploy on her part. But that sacrifice was unnecessary. Stupid girl. I could have muddled through on my own, and she could have kept her baron."

Sebastian finally spoke up. "We are better off knowing that he's a disloyal arse. If he can't stand by her in a moment like that, he doesn't deserve her."

"While I cannot argue with your logic, Grey, I still wish the chit had kept quiet. She has destroyed many of her opportunities with what she did."

Wesley felt the earl's eyes boring into him as he paced. Finally, he turned to him, raising his eyebrows. "Do you have something to add?"

"Do you really think she should be tied for life to some bounder who cannot bother to ascertain the truthfulness of a situation?"

"No, but surely you both realize that everything about the Marriage Mart is about appearances. Loyalty and all that come later. Most noblemen expect their wives to be virtuously unassailable. By publicly declaring that we spent time alone on the terrace, Anne called her own virtue into question. While we all know nothing questionable happened, she caused speculation to rise, which will drastically alter how she is perceived. I am unsure if the three of us are in any position to help her straighten this out given our own reputations."

The other two looked momentarily uncomfortable but then shrugged over the inevitability of the situation. The earl spoke up. "No use in worrying over it now. Let us reconvene on the morrow."

"At least one of us needs to call on her tomorrow. I am unsure if it should be me." Wesley couldn't decide if it would do more harm than good.

"I would be happy to do so," Sebastian offered.

"Very well, then come meet us at the club to let us know how she goes on."

~~~

"Before you ask me anything, I need a drink first," Sebastian declared as soon as he arrived to meet his friends.

Wesley waited impatiently while his friend threw back his first glass. "Well, how is she?" Sebastian had barely swallowed. Wesley needed to know Anne was all right.

"She appeared to be fairly well rested and was quite in her looks, to be honest with you. But the situation is dire, in my opinion."
~~~

"Why? What happened? Did she have no callers?"

"She had plenty of callers, they just were of a much different nature than previously."

"What do you mean? Get to your point, man."

Sebastian grinned at Wesley's impatience, despite the situation they faced. "There were no young ladies calling on her, for one thing. And for another, the gentlemen were of the nature of Lord Samson."

"Samson? Doesn't he have seven or eight children and he's looking for his fourth wife?"

"The very one."

"But he's got to be headed for sixty," the earl pointed out.

"Besides the fact that he's looking for an unpaid governess for his passel of children rather than a proper wife," Wesley added with disgust. "Anne needs a husband who will cherish her, not one who's looking for a nursemaid."

"And he was actually one of the better callers. I didn't want to tell you about some of the others."

"Why? Who else was there?" Wesley demanded, feeling as though his blood were turning cold.

Sebastian couldn't even look him in the eye as he answered with one word. "Patterson."

"Patterson?" Wesley was confused for a moment. "But he's not in the market for a wife."

"Exactly," Sebastian said just before Wesley exploded out of his chair.

"What could that bounder be thinking, soiling an innocent young debutante with his presence? Lady Sophie allowed him entrance?" He was incredulous.

"You know how lax Lady Sophie has been. And poor Lady Anne would have no knowledge of him, so she wouldn't know to tell the butler not to admit him." Sebastian took another gulp of his brandy, as though to wash the bad taste from his mouth.

"We have to go over there and talk some sense into that chit." Wesley was on his way to the door when Lord Spencer stopped him.

"Dunbar, wait. What do you think you will be able to accomplish? You're the reason the girl is in this mess. I suspect you ought to stay far away from Lady Anne and let her relatives sort this out."

Wesley knew the earl was making sense, but he just couldn't bear to stand by and do nothing. He said as much to his friends. "We have to be able to do something. We got her into this." He saw the sardonic look on the others' faces and amended his words. "All right, I got her into this mess as you said, but we have to be able to do something. Obviously, her relatives are inattentive and unreliable. We cannot just leave her to the wolves. There has to be something we can do."

"For the moment, there is nothing that can be done. Is it not tonight that you are to host her at the theatre? That will be the perfect time for you to talk to her and see how she is faring. Perhaps her baron will still come up to scratch, and there is nothing to for us to be worrying about." Wesley recognized Spencer's soothing tone and it put his teeth on edge.

His low rumble of disgust sounded almost like a growl, but there was nothing else for him to do. Wesley nodded at his two friends and left. He had every intention of going home, but he soon discovered himself asking Lady Sophie's butler if he might speak with Lady Anne for a few moments. The butler looked dubious but allowed him to enter and then left him cooling his heels in the receiving room while he went to see if my lady was at home to visitors.

~~~

The day thus far had been an unmitigated disaster. None of Anne's usual callers had shown their faces, but that did not mean the knocker had remained silent. *No, that would have been a delight*, Anne thought with an edge of hysteria creeping into her
~~~

mind. A shudder shivered down her back at the thought of that afternoon's callers. She should have said she wasn't going to accept callers as she had intended. Spending the entire day in bed would have been far preferable to how the day had turned out. Perhaps it was time to retire from Society. She ought to send a note to Lord Dunbar declining his invitation for the theatre. That thought brought a pang of regret. She had been so looking forward to the treat but under the circumstances, she was unsure if she could face going out in public.

She was just about to dissolve into tears when there was a knock on her door. It distracted her just enough to prevent the tears from spilling over her eyelashes. She opened the door to find a footman waiting with a message summoning her to the morning room.

"Who has sent the summons?" she asked, wondering over the footman's choice of words.

"I apologize for not being more clear, my lady. Your aunt has sent for you."

"Thank you, Jason. I shall be right there." She closed the door and ran to her vanity to check her appearance. After running a comb through her hair, she decided she needn't make any other alterations and hurried to do her aunt's bidding. Hopefully the older lady would have some direction to help get her out of the mess she had created.

Her feet froze to the floor immediately upon stepping into the morning room. She could barely believe her eyes.

"Papa?" she asked, almost at a shout, before running and throwing herself into his arms. She could not bring herself to let him go, so all the questions she was asking were muffled by his coat.

Lord Austen laughed and pulled his daughter out of his arms. "Anne, my dear girl, I cannot make out anything that you're saying. Surely, I have not been gone so very long to generate a reaction like that. Now what were you asking?"

Anne couldn't help herself; she threw herself back into his arms but contented herself with one tight squeeze and then pulled herself away.

"It may not have been so very long, Papa, but you didn't say where you were going or when you would be back, so I was becoming quite alarmed over your absence. But never mind, you're here now and I am so happy to see you."

Anne took a deep breath and looked around the room, becoming aware of the strained silence amongst the other occupants. She felt the heat climbing into her cheeks as she realized that a stranger was also present. She dipped into a hurried curtsy.

"I am so sorry, my lady, I did not realize you had a caller, I was just that happy to see my father."

Lady Sophie looked discomfited, but it was apparently not directed at Anne as she shook her head and patted the seat next to her. "Of course, my dear, pay it no mind but come and take a seat here beside me."

Anne was confused over her aunt's strange tone but did as she was bid. After she settled herself carefully on the settee, she looked at the unknown woman and wondered why the room was so silent. She offered the woman as friendly a smile as she could muster given her own discomfort.

When still no one said anything, Anne transferred her gaze to her father. When their gazes met, her father's eyes widened.

"I apologize, my dear, I have forgotten my manners, please, allow me to introduce to you Mrs. Appleton. She has done me the honour of agreeing to be my wife."

Anne blinked a few times, wondering if she had somehow become stuck in a strange dream, but then her good breeding clicked on and she went through the motions of polite behaviour. She stood and curtsied briefly to the other woman before taking her hand and saying, "How do you do?" She wasn't sure why her aunt was being so strange about the woman. She didn't look to be completely ineligible. Anne wondered if it might have to do with thoughts of her late sister but dismissed that thought as she hadn't gotten the impression the two sisters were even all that close. Anne braced herself for what was sure to be an uncomfortable experience.

"How did the two of you meet?" she asked politely, wondering what the proper protocol for becoming acquainted with one's future stepmother was. She could tell the other woman was uncomfortable, but Anne wasn't sure how to make her feel at ease.

Lord Austen jumped in to answer when it became apparent Mrs. Appleton wasn't going to say anything. "She was an angel of mercy when I fell into difficulty. I couldn't help but fall in love with her."

Anne hoped her smile wasn't too wan as she looked at the pair. "How lovely."

Lady Sophie got to her feet. "Well, shall I have my housekeeper make up a room?"

"Oh, no, my lady, my companion and I will be staying at Nerot's Hotel. We merely wished to stop by and meet Lord Austen's daughter." Mrs. Appleton turned to Anne and continued, "I know you must be rather busy with all the activities of your first Season, but I do hope we can become better acquainted before we leave for Rowanwood. Lord Austen is hoping to resume escorting you, and I'm sure you have a lot to catch up on."

Lady Sophie did not wait for Anne to reply. "Well, this evening we have a commitment that does not include Lord Austen and for which we ought to begin our preparations. It was a pleasure to make your acquaintance." With those words, she swept from the room without a backward glance.

Anne stood staring blankly at the door through which her aunt had just left, unsure how she ought to proceed. She looked at her father and his betrothed uncertainly.

Her father, surprising Anne with his astuteness, launched into speech. "Do not worry about your aunt, my dear, and do not worry that we are troubled by her. Lady Sophie does not take well to change. But she is a good woman and will come around. Now, go ahead and get ready. I will be staying here. Perhaps over breakfast in the morning we can make plans to spend some time together."

"Very well." Anne didn't know how else to reply. She kissed her father on the cheek and shook Mrs. Appleton's hand before leaving the room. "I look forward to getting to know you, ma'am," she added with as sincere a smile as she could muster given the strange events of the past day.

Just as she neared the foyer and the stairs up to her room, the butler stopped her.

"My lady, I was unsure if I should disturb you with this matter, but Lord Dunbar has called to see you. He is in the receiving room."

Anne felt her heart sink and yet its rate at least doubled if not tripled while butterflies took flight in her stomach. She bit her lip with uncertainty. The butler must have interpreted this to mean she did not wish to see the viscount.

"I will demand that he vacate the premises."

"No, no, that is unnecessary, but thank you for the offer. I will see to him. I will ring for you if I need you." Anne was not feeling at all prepared to face the viscount, but she could not bear to have him evicted from the house either. She stopped outside the receiving room, took a deep breath, rubbed her now clammy hands over her skirt, glancing down to make sure it was free of creases or wrinkles. Throwing back her shoulders and lifting her chin, she entered the room, hoping she looked far more confident than she felt.

"Good afternoon, my lord, how pleasant to see you." She almost smiled with delight over how composed she sounded.

"My lady, I trust I have not disturbed you overly. I did not realize it would take so long for the butler to find you."

The viscount's words, although censorious, set her at ease, and she actually laughed. "I'm sorry, my lord, were you waiting long? I must admit the house is a little at sixes and sevens, but you should not have been left to cool your heels. Please, accept my apologies."

"No, no apologies necessary, I am just glad to see that you are all right." The viscount's searching gaze examined her face, making Anne a trifle uncomfortable, but she tried to keep her face impassive as she bore up under the scrutiny.

Finally, just as she thought she could bear it no longer, the viscount strode toward her. "Ach, Anne, it is I who owe you an apology. I thought I could play god with your life, and now I've just made a mess of it. I should have left well enough alone from the beginning."

Anne's eyes welled with tears as he grasped her hands warmly in his. "But then I would not have had your friendship, my lord, and I cannot regret that."

"But that friendship led you to do something rather stupid, did it not?"

A watery chuckle escaped her lips as she nodded and then shrugged. "It would appear that none of those people were really my friends anyway, since you are the only one who has turned up today. Well except for Lord Grey, but he looked sorely pained for being here."

"Well, that was because you were so daft as to allow entrance to ones such as Samson and Patterson."

Anne's tears dried up as her anger surged. "How was I supposed to know they were such unsavoury fellows? No one had seen fit to warn me about them nor mention to the butler that they were not to be admitted."

"Why is your aunt never around?" The viscount did not seem to be put off by her angry outburst but was genuinely curious about his question.

Anne sighed. "I cannot explain my confusing family, my lord."

By now the two had seated themselves on the settee. Lord Dunbar still held one of her hands in his grasp. Anne was unsure what to do with her other one. It was highly irregular, but she quite enjoyed the warmth spreading through her from where her hand rested in his and did not wish to end the encounter just yet.

"Will you still come to the theatre tonight?"

"If you are still willing to have me, my lord, I am still anxious to see the performance."

"Of course, I still want you to come. I don't care a fig for the thoughts of the *ton*. You have done nothing wrong and ought to keep your head held high."

"Do you think I can brazen it out, my lord?"

"I think you can and you should," he replied stoutly.

They sat in silence for a moment.

"My father has returned."

"Oh, good."

"He brought his betrothed with him."

The viscount's hand tightened over hers. "He is getting married?" He appeared incredulous.

"It would seem so, my lord. They did not say if they had already set a date. I have a feeling they might be waiting for me to be settled. If that is the case, they might have to wait for a while."

"Is that why you said things were at sixes and sevens when I arrived?"

Anne nodded. "My aunt seems to be taking it hard. I cannot understand why. Mrs. Appleton seems acceptable enough. I have not had a chance to get to know her, of course, but she did not appear to be terribly *déclassé* or grasping."

"Would you like me to invite them for this evening?"

Anne felt her cheeks warming over his question. "That is so kind of you to ask, my lord. Would you think less of me if I say no?"

Lord Dunbar laughed. "Not at all, but I do want to know why."

She felt her cheeks reddening further. "I wish to be able to enjoy the play. It will be hard enough with my own precarious position. If I have to think about my father and his friend, I shall be so distracted there won't be any point in even attending the theatre tonight."

"I understand completely. Pay it no mind, my dear, I only offered as a favour to you anyway."

Anne laughed and rose to her feet. "Well, my lord, I hate to be rude and ask you to leave, but I do have an engagement at the theatre this evening, so I need to be making my preparations."

The viscount rose to his feet as well. Laughing, he pinched her chin. "You are turning into a minx, my dear. I shall see you later." He raised her hand to his lips, placing a kiss gently on her wrist.

Anne turned on her heel and left the room without saying anything further. She felt the tingling in her arm all the way up to her chamber. As she shut the door, she turned and leaned on it. She knew she was being foolish, but she so wished the viscount was not so set on maintaining his bachelor status.

With a sigh, she rang for her maid to help her get ready for the evening.

Chapter Fourteen

The play was well along, and Anne was oblivious to anything around her as all her attention was centred on the stage. Wesley was glad of that as he watched how little attention she was receiving from the assembled audience. Or rather how much veiled attention she was receiving. At least she seemed to be oblivious to it as she sat enraptured by the spectacle on stage. For his part, he had no idea what the play was about. All his attention was on her and what he could do about her situation.

The good news was, she wasn't ruined. No one had given her the cut direct. But no one had stopped by his box to greet her either. The only bright side to that was that he didn't have to plant any of those bounders a facer. If either Samson or Patterson had wanted to speak with her, he would not have been fully responsible for his actions, he thought with a grimace.

Anne had been radiant when she arrived with her aunt at his box at the appointed time. Despite her nerves about being out in public after the debacle the night before, her excitement over finally getting to the theatre had kept her from appearing pale. She was always gracious, so she had politely greeted the other guests he had assembled and made brief conversation before the curtain had been raised. Since then, she had sat mute in her chair at the front of the box with her attention never wavering from the performance.

It was a novelty to see someone actually paying attention to the show. So many of the wellborn audience attended the theatre to watch one another rather than the stage. But not Lady Anne, he was delighted to observe.

When the intermission arrived, he watched her blink as though awaking from a trance. He hid his amusement.

"That was amazing," she enthused. "Thank you so very much, my lord, for having us this evening. I am enjoying myself immensely."

"I am glad. Would you like me to have a footman fetch you some refreshments during the intermission, or would you like to take a stroll?"

He was saddened to see her shrink back slightly in her chair at the thought. "No, thank you, I think I shall just sit here and enjoy the experience."

Wesley had a footman go collect a selection of options anyway; he figured the other guests would appreciate some refreshments even if Anne refused. Most of his guests filed out of the box to stretch their legs for a few minutes. Lady Sophie remained to lend countenance to her niece, but she was entrenched in a conversation with one of her cronies, who happened to be in the box next to his.

Taking a seat next to Anne, Wesley engaged her in conversation.

"Is it as good as you had expected?"

"I really didn't know quite what to expect, so I will say that it is even better than I expected." She answered him with a grin that caused his chest to tighten slightly. He ignored the sensation as best he could.

"Is your aunt any more resolved to your father's betrothal?" he next asked, keeping his voice low.

Anne's quiet chuckle surprised him. "If by resolved you mean pretending the situation does not exist, then yes." She cast her eyes back at her aunt to ensure she was still not paying attention. "I don't know what to make of it, my lord." She then heaved a quiet sigh.

"Why the sigh, my lady?"

"I feel dreadful for thinking of myself in the face of my father's happiness, but when everything came crashing down last night, I had been comforting myself with the thought that I can at least return to Rowanwood with my father and make an attempt to repair our circumstances. I feel quite prepared to work hard and turn things around. But now it seems he intends to do that work with someone else, and I shall be in the way. It rather leaves me with very few options." She looked Wesley in the eyes, and her next question made him feel as though she had punched him in the gut. "Do you think Lord Samson would be truly dreadful? My heart does go out to all those motherless children."

"You are not going to wed the likes of Samson, my lady. Not if I have any say over the matter."

"But you really do not have any say, do you, my lord? You are just my friend and really, this needn't concern you. I need to arrange a future for myself, and it would seem that my options are narrowing."

Wesley was about to reply when the signal came that the performance was about to resume. The others filed back into the box, and Lady Sophie fluttered around and settled next to Anne. No more conversation would be possible.

Once again, Anne's attention was snared by the actors on the stage and she was no longer aware of what was going on around her. It was a good thing because Wesley's mood took a noted dive as he became aware of Lord Patterson staring intently at Anne. Wesley had no wish for another scene, but he felt himself mentally daring the man to approach. His protective urges toward Anne knew no bounds.

As the curtain fell on the final scene, Anne's enthusiastic clapping filled the box. Wesley grinned as the others joined in; most of them had been caught up in conversations and had barely noticed that the performance was over.

Anne's warm smile encompassed everyone nearby as she declared, "Was that not the most delightful experience ever?"

Lady Sophie chuckled at her niece. "Not particularly, my dear. Your lack of experience is showing, but that's all right, it is rather endearing."

Wesley's heart clutched as he saw Anne's crestfallen expression after her aunt's callous words. Her confused glance met his, and he offered her an encouraging smile. Her chin rose and he could see her determination bolstered. She ignored her aunt's statement.

"Well, I rather enjoyed it and I am glad we came."

As they were leaving Wesley's box, Lord Patterson stepped up unacceptably close to Anne. Even though Wesley was right behind her, he could not hear what the wicked man said to her. He could not bear to see the bounder's hand on her.

"I would ask that you remove yourself from my future wife's presence, Patterson, you are not welcome here. And I would demand that you not approach her again in the future."

Wesley heard a couple audible gasps as those around who had heard him processed what he had said. He was happy to note that none of them originated with Anne. She merely looked at him with serious, widened eyes from a pale face. She did not look pleased, but she did not gainsay him either. Wesley had not been led to believe that Anne's aunt was very bright, but she quickly assessed the situation and bustled Anne away from the gathering crowd.

The Earl of Sutton quickly took his position next to Wesley, but the show of solidarity didn't seem to be necessary. Patterson looked at the two of them and bowed slightly.

"My apologies, Dunbar, I had no idea the wind blew in that direction."

"Now you know, so get yourself off."

Patterson turned on his heel, and the crowd dispersed with a rumble of disappointment that there wasn't to be more of a scene.

Wesley looked around and was disappointed to feel abandoned when he realized Anne was nowhere in sight.

"Her aunt got her away before there was any possibility of a crush," the earl supplied when he saw Wesley's searching gaze. "And might I ask, when did this develop?"

Wesley's jaw was cramping from clenching it so tight. "It hasn't, yet. I just couldn't bear to see her evening ruined by the likes of Patterson."

"So, you announced that she is your betrothed?" Lord Spencer was incredulous.

Wesley shrugged and offered his friend a shamefaced smile. "A little bit of overkill perhaps, but the matter is now settled."

"But now you will have to marry the girl."

"I know." Wesley was amazed at how right that felt.

"How do you think she is going to feel about it?"

"Would it make me an arrogant monster to say that she will probably be delighted?"

"Yes."

The two men shared a chuckle as they left the theatre and proceeded to their club to drink to the future couple's happiness.

~~~

Anne got very little sleep that night and was up early pacing in her room the next morning. She had been unable to choke down much breakfast and was wringing her hands uselessly when she heard the door knocker sound. She hoped and dreaded equally if it were the viscount.

The footman soon ended her suspense. Indeed, the Viscount of Bracondale had called to speak to her father and asked that she be summoned shortly. Anne was swept with a wave of fury that put the run to the pallor she had earlier seen in the mirror. She swept down to the receiving room and paced there until she heard her father's voice.

"Ah, my dear girl, the butler mentioned you were waiting for us here. How delightful that we shall both be wed before the Season is over."
~~~

Her face felt tight as she smiled briefly at her father. He obviously wanted her to be happy with this development, and she had no wish to disappoint him. He seemed oblivious to her distress. Anne could tell from the viscount's searching gaze that he was much more aware of her volatile mood.

Her father was still talking. "I would assume the two of you have plenty to discuss, so I will allow you a few minutes of privacy." He left the room, leaving the door ajar for a semblance of respectability.

"You do not look pleased," Wesley commented, prompting a derisive snort from Anne.

"Pleased? No, Lord Dunbar, I am not surprised to hear you say that, as I am decidedly not pleased."

She was almost amused by the surprised look that flitted across the viscount's face before he once again was looking at her with his impassive face hiding his thoughts. "Would you care to tell me why? I would have thought you would think it the perfect solution."

"I have no idea what gave you that idea, my lord. You were quite clear on the subject. You would rather throw me to the wolves than make an offer for me. Well, I would rather be ruined than be tied for the rest of my life to a man that would threaten me like that. And I most certainly do not wish to be married to someone who has been forced into it."

"I have not been forced," Wesley insisted hotly before continuing with his tone cooling. "Would you have rather I left you to the tender mercies of Lord Patterson?"

"No, I would have rather you had left it well enough alone. I could have handled him." She paced a few steps away from the viscount before whirling back to face him. "Don't you see? All I ever wanted was to find a comfortable partner to start a new life with. You have no desire to be married. How are we ever going to be comfortable together?"

Anne blinked as she watched the viscount's impassive expression disappear to be replaced by one of warm admiration. "I hate to disagree with you, my dear, but I really have to argue with you. While you are quite correct that up until now I have had no desire to find myself leg shackled, I find I cannot face the thought of you being wedded to anyone else. That leaves me to conclude that I am quite determined to have you for myself." A look of uncertainty crossed his face, much to Anne's delight. "That is, if you will have me."

Anne crossed her arms to prevent them from being thrown around him. She tried to maintain a severe expression. "How do I know you are serious?"

"I promise you, I am absolutely serious. I will promise to give up all my profligate ways. I know you want to live a quiet life, so I will promise we can move to one of my country estates and raise chickens if that will make you happy."

Anne chortled. "Chickens?" She wrinkled her nose. "I think they are rather nasty creatures if you must know." She laughed again. "That was a lovely speech, but I fear you will be bored within a week if I were to take you up on the offer."

"No, I swear to you, I shan't be bored as long as you are by my side. Besides, you cannot make me eat my words to Patterson."

With another laugh, this time bordering on a giggle, Anne finally allowed the viscount to take her hands and draw her close. "You don't care a single jot for Patterson, so don't think you can bamboozle me. What must Lord Grey and Lord Spencer think? They will have my head for this."

"They shall have to go through me first."

Anne gazed at the viscount with a measured stare. "Are you absolutely certain you could bear it, my lord?"

"It is my heart's desire. I swear it to you."

Anne finally relented and threw herself into his arms. "Very well, I shall be your wife. But I shan't hold you to your promises of country living, my lord, as I am quite convinced you would go mad. Perhaps we could find a good compromise of town and country."

"You are the most managing little baggage I have ever proposed to."

She giggled again. "I am the only one you have proposed to, so that's not too difficult." Further conversation was stifled as he drew her in to seal their bargain with a kiss.

Epilogue

Anne could barely sit still. Wesley's sigh nearly pushed her over, and a fit of giggles overcame her.

"Your fake sighs only serve to make me laugh, my lord," she pointed out.

"Then they have served their purpose, my dear." Wesley returned her fond gaze. "But explain to me again why we were going to ensconce ourselves in the country for a fortnight."

"For one thing, because you love me," Anne answered with a saucy smile.

"That I do, but what's the other thing?"

Anne's sigh was genuine and filled with joy. "Because we have friends who would like to spend time with us."

"Oh, yes, that." Wesley grinned.

"It is due to the Duke and Duchess of Wrentham that we found each other. And since you've always claimed he was your best friend, you ought to be glad we're going to see him."

"Really, you could argue that it is because of Sir Broderick that we found each other. He was quite the matchmaker for such a villain, wouldn't you say?"

"That he was. It's a pity he's no longer around to gnash his teeth in despair. I can't imagine one such as him would rejoice with us."

They shared another loving glance before Wesley continued with his complaint. "You know I have no complaint about seeing Alex and Rose. But do you think they'll require us to call them your grace?"

Anne laughed. "It would be the polite thing to do. At least Lord and Lady Sinclair will be there as well, so you shan't be alone."

"But all either couple will want to discuss is their infants." Wesley's disgust with the coming two weeks was evident.

"That might be true, but you should try to listen closely," Anne answered with a soft smile and a delicate gesture toward her own midsection.

Ever sharp-eyed, Wesley's gaze narrowed on his wife. "Are you trying to tell me something? Or trying to avoid telling me something?"

Anne laughed, joy clear in the sound. "I was planning to wait a little longer just to be certain, but I'm fairly sure you'll soon be irritating Grey and Spencer with your own conversations."

Wesley pulled her into his arms to demonstrate to her just how happy he was with her news.

"I knew the moment you turned those defiant kitten eyes on me after Alex and Rose disappeared that you were going to turn my life around."

Anne burst into laughter. "Turn it on its head, you mean."

"It needed turning, my dear. It wasn't right until you turned up into it."

They could feel the carriage slowing and turning into the drive to Heath, and they faced forward, looking into a very happy future.

The End

About the Author

I've been writing pretty much since I learned to read when I was five years old. Of course, those early efforts were basically only something a mother could love :-). I put writing aside after I left school and stuck with reading. I am an avid reader. I love words. I will read anything, even the cereal box, signs, posters, etc. But my true love is novels.

Almost ten years ago my husband dared me to write a book instead of always reading them. I didn't think I'd be able to do it, but to my surprise I love writing. Those early efforts eventually became my first published book – Tempting the Earl (published by Avalon Books in 2010). There were some ups and downs in my publishing efforts. My first publisher was sold and I became an "orphan" author, back to the drawing board of trying to find a publishing house. It has been a thrilling adventure as I learned to navigate the world of publishing.

I believe firmly that everyone deserves a happily ever after. I want my readers to be able to escape from the everyday for a little while and feel upbeat and refreshed when they get to the end of my books.

When not reading or writing, I can be found traipsing around my neighborhood admiring the dogs and greenery or travelling the world with my favorite companion.

Stay in touch:

www.wendymayandrews.com

www.facebook.com/WendyMayAndrews

www.instagram.com/WendyMayAndrews

www.twitter.com/WendyMayAndrews

Have you read the first two books in this series?

The Duke Conspiracy

Anything is possible with a spying debutante, a duke, and a conspiracy.

Growing up, Rose and Alex were the best of friends until their families became embroiled in a feud. Now, the Season is throwing them into each other's company. Despite the spark of attraction they might feel for one another, they each want very different things in life, besides needing to support their own family's side in the dispute.

Miss Rosamund Smythe is finding the Season to be a dead bore after spying with her father, a baron diplomat, in Vienna. She wants more out of life than just being some nobleman's wife. When she overhears a plot to entrap Alex into a marriage of convenience, her intrigue and some last vestige of loyalty causes them to overcome the feud.

His Grace, Alexander Milton, the Duke of Wrentham, wants a quiet life with a "proper" wife after his tumultuous childhood. His parents had fought viciously, lied often, and Alex had hated it all.

Rose's meddling puts her in danger. Alex will have to leave the simple peace he craves to claim a love he never could have imagined. Can they claim their happily ever after despite the turmoil?

Available through Amazon

Find out what happens to Elizabeth after Rose is kidnapped from the ball in the exciting sequel,

The Countess Intrigue

Engaged to a rumored murderer. What's a lady to do?

During her second Season, Lady Elizabeth Castleton is found in a compromising situation with Lord Justice Sinclair, the Earl of Heath. Despite her attraction to him, she is dismayed to find herself betrothed to the man who is rumored to have killed his first wife. Her parents refuse to lend credence to the rumors, so she is soon married and on the way to her husband's estate.

She cannot decide what to make of the handsome earl but after an attempt is made on her life, Elizabeth is terrified that history is about to repeat itself. She determines to find out once and for all if she is married to a murderer.

Can she stay alive long enough to find her happily ever after?

Available through Amazon

If you've enjoyed the Mayfair Mayhem series, you might also enjoy another regency series by Wendy May Andrews,

The Ladies of Mayfair.

Enjoy reading:

The Governess' Debut

The governess must charm both the spoiled child and the haughty earl.

Orphaned and destitute, gently born Felicia Scott must find a way to keep a roof over her head. No longer able to enter the Marriage Mart, but also not of the servant class, the only option is to find a position as governess.

After his spoiled, seven year old daughter has sent off three governesses in the 18 months since her mother died, the Earl of Standish doubts the young, inexperienced Miss Scott could possible manage the position. Since he's desperate and she comes so highly recommended, the earl agrees to give her a chance. Much to everyone's amazement, the beautiful, young governess succeeds where the others had failed. The entire household benefits from the calm, including the jaded earl.

How does he overcome his arrogance to see his governess' true value?

Available through Amazon

Manufactured by Amazon.ca
Bolton, ON